THE SISTER'S GRIMM

⑦

THE S...
GR...

10th Anniversary Edition

7

THE EVERAFTER WAR

MICHAEL BUCKLEY

Pictures by PETER FERGUSON

AMULET BOOKS   NEW YORK

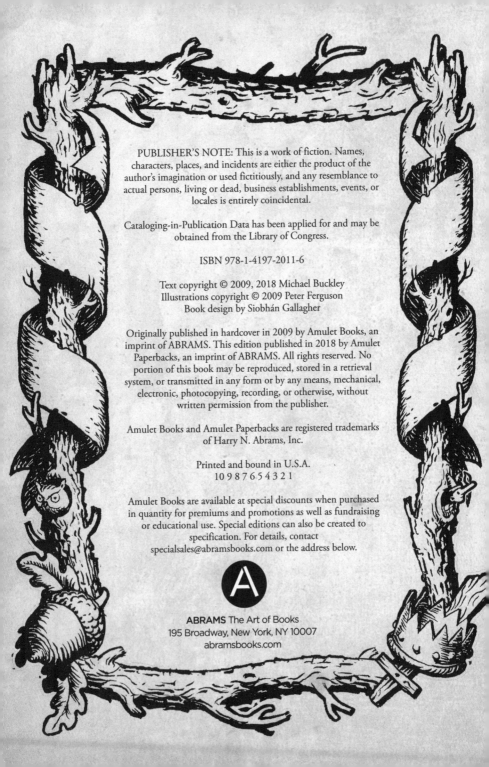

Cataloging-in-Publication Data has been applied for and may be obtained from the Library of Congress.

ISBN 978-1-4197-2011-6

Text copyright © 2009, 2018 Michael Buckley
Illustrations copyright © 2009 Peter Ferguson
Book design by Siobhán Gallagher

Printed and bound in U.S.A.
10 9 8 7 6 5 4 3 2 1

Amulet Books are available at special discounts when purchased in quantity for premiums and promotions as well as fundraising or educational use. Special editions can also be created to specification. For details, contact specialsales@abramsbooks.com or the address below.

ABRAMS The Art of Books
195 Broadway, New York, NY 10007
abramsbooks.com

For my brother, Edwin

Y ou?! You're the Master? You're the leader of the Scarlet Hand?" Sabrina cried.

"Yes," he replied calmly.

She stood aghast, shocked by the betrayal. Disgust, rage, and terror filled her head and heart, sending confusing signals to every part of her body. One moment she wanted to run—to put as much distance between herself and the villain as possible. The next, she wanted to grab him by the collar and shake him until he explained himself and his deception.

"But you—" Daphne started, trembling.

"But I was your friend?" he asked. "Is that what you were going to say?"

"I trusted you," Daphne said.

"We all trusted you!" Sabrina spat.

He shook his head as if he couldn't believe their foolishness.

"I'm afraid you've made a terrible mistake."

1

Six Days Earlier

SABRINA GRIMM'S LIFE WAS A COLLECTION OF peculiar, almost unbelievable events. But, sitting in her grandmother's living room with three massive brown bears had to be the most peculiar of all.

The bears in question had arrived with a blond, curly-haired woman. She was a beauty, with a big smile, dimples in both cheeks, and a dainty nose sprinkled with freckles. Her name was Goldilocks. Yes, *the* Goldilocks, but all grown up and overflowing with nervous energy. She kept rushing around the living room rearranging things. She moved lamps and rugs, switched furniture around, and even rehung family portraits on different walls. When she moved something, she would step back and study it, mutter something incomprehensible to herself, and then move it again. Once she finally liked where it landed, she would beam with pride and say, "Just right."

Sabrina watched Goldilocks from a love seat across the room. Her little sister, Daphne, sat next to her, chewing on her palm—a quirky habit she slipped into when she was very excited or happy. At their feet sat the Grimm family's two-hundred-pound Great Dane, Elvis. He turned his big head back and forth from Sabrina and Daphne to the bears and Goldilocks. Every few seconds he let out a soft, confused whine. Sabrina understood how he felt.

"Just another day in Ferryport Landing, Elvis," she muttered, then turned to her sister. "How long are we going to wait?"

Daphne shrugged. "Granny said she'd come downstairs to get us as soon as she could. Maybe we should offer them something to eat, to be polite."

"Like what? A trout?"

Goldilocks grunted and huffed, and the bears responded with a series of short grunts. They seemed to be talking with one another, but Sabrina couldn't understand any of it. When they finished up their odd chat, Goldilocks told Sabrina that the biggest of the bears would love a cup of Earl Grey tea, very hot. The second biggest would prefer iced tea. The littlest would like some chocolate milk, if it wasn't too much trouble.

Sabrina was bewildered. Growing up in New York City, she had witnessed people speaking to animals on more than one occasion. Once, on the subway, she'd overheard a heated discussion between a man and a one-eyed mutt about Napoleon's defeat at Waterloo. But, in Ferryport Landing, animals talked back.

"We'll be right back," Daphne promised, pulling her sister into the kitchen with Elvis in tow. There, they found a little girl in red pajamas huddled in a corner. Her sad, shy face was framed with amber curls that tumbled across her shoulders. Sabrina immediately wished she had stayed in the living room with the bears. Only yesterday, Red Riding Hood had been a deranged maniac. Now that she was supposedly cured, Granny had invited her to live with them. Sabrina wondered if she'd ever get used to seeing Red's face.

"Are they gone yet?" Red whispered.

"No," Daphne said. "But they're friends, Red. You don't have to hide."

Red didn't look convinced. She tried to squeeze deeper into the corner.

Daphne went to work preparing the drinks while Sabrina spied on their guests through the crack in the kitchen door. Goldilocks continued to rush around the living room reorganizing everything. The bears sat listlessly on the couch. If it wasn't so strange, it might have been boring.

"Goldilocks is giving me a headache," Sabrina admitted. "Why can't she sit still?"

"Don't spy," Daphne scolded. "It's rude."

"Aren't you curious about her? Dad was in love with her before he met Mom." Sabrina studied the woman. Goldilocks was very pretty, and she seemed nice enough. But she was also exhausting. She couldn't relax. Plus, she was no Veronica Grimm. Sabrina's mom was a knockout.

"Love is weird," Daphne said with a hint of authority.

Sabrina laughed. "And you're an expert? You're only—" She stopped herself when she spotted her sister's scowl. Sabrina was already treading on thin ice with Daphne. "Yeah, you're right. Love is weird."

"Red, won't you please join us?" Daphne asked kindly, when the drinks were ready.

Red shook her head vigorously, staring down at the floor.

The sisters carried the tray of drinks into the living room.

"This is a bad idea," Goldilocks fretted. She sat on the ottoman, only to jump up again, rush across the room, and move a vase an inch to the left. "I shouldn't have come here. Your father is not going to be happy."

"He'll understand. We've tried everything we can think of to wake them up. You're our last hope," Sabrina said, nearly panicked that the woman might change her mind.

Goldilocks went to work rearranging the books in the family's massive bookshelves.

"I tried to respect his wishes. I moved to New York City and lived there for a long time. I had a nice little apartment in the East

Village. Even when I heard he and Veronica moved to Manhattan, I never went to see him. I avoided the fairy kingdom in Central Park in case he ever went there. It was my way of showing that I was sorry for what happened to his dad, and now, here I am, breaking my promise to stay out of his life. When he opens his eyes and sees me standing over him, he's going to be furious. And your mother! She's going to think I'm a . . . a harlot!"

"What's *harlot* mean?" Daphne asked.

"A harlot is—" Sabrina started.

"I asked Goldilocks, not you," Daphne snapped.

Sabrina's face flushed at the sharp tone. It stung that Daphne wanted as little to do with her as possible.

"A harlot is a woman with a bad reputation. A harlot is a woman who kisses another woman's husband," Goldilocks explained, then turned to Momma Bear. "What do you think I should do?"

Momma Bear shrugged.

"A lot of help you are!" Goldilocks scolded, then turned back to Daphne. "What is keeping your grandmother?"

"Same old Goldie," a voice sang from across the room. Sabrina turned to find Uncle Jake, wearing his trench coat with hundreds of extra pockets sewn into it and a huge smile. "Just as impatient as I remember. You should see her in a drive-thru restaurant, girls. Fast food isn't fast enough for her."

Goldilocks frowned and moved a paperweight from the coffee

table to the bureau. "Jake Grimm! Don't tease me. I'm a nervous wreck."

"Then let's get this show on the road," he said, gesturing toward the stairs. "We're all ready."

Goldilocks bit her lower lip and followed Jake, the bears and Sabrina and Daphne close behind. Unfortunately, the girls found themselves downwind of the bears' special brand of funk.

Granny Relda was waiting at the top of the stairs. She was a stout woman with wrinkles lining her face. She wore a bright white dress and a matching hat with a sunflower appliqué in its center. She grinned and embraced Goldilocks as if she were one of her own children.

"It's good to see you, Goldie," she said in her light German accent. Granny had grown up in Berlin and moved to America when she married the girls' late grandfather, Basil.

Goldilocks smiled and nearly cried at the same time. "It's been a long time, Mrs. Grimm."

"Who is Mrs. Grimm? Call me Relda, honey," she said, then turned to Sabrina. "Where is our friend Red?"

"Being weird in the kitchen."

"Red!" the old woman called out, and a few moments later the little girl appeared at the bottom of the steps.

"Are you coming?" the old woman asked.

Red shook her head. "This is your family. I don't belong."

Granny gestured for her to join them. "Come along, *liebling*."

Reluctantly, Red climbed the stairs, and Granny led everyone into a spare bedroom furnished with a mirror and a queen-size bed. Lying comfortably on the mattress were Sabrina and Daphne's parents, Henry and Veronica Grimm. Both were deeply asleep, enchanted by a spell that would not allow them to wake up. Granny Relda took Henry's hand.

Goldie looked like she was about to faint. She leaned against the bedroom wall for support. "Relda, I—"

Granny Relda waved her off. "There's nothing to apologize for. What happened to Basil was not your fault. It wasn't anyone's fault."

Sabrina watched Uncle Jake's gaze drift to the floor. She wondered if he would ever forgive himself for his part in Basil's death.

"I appreciate your kindness, but I'm not sure Henry feels the same way," Goldie said. "How long have they been like this?"

"They were kidnapped two years ago," Daphne explained. "We only got them back a few months ago. So far as we know, they've been like this the whole time."

"Did you try Prince Charming?" Goldilocks said. "He has a knack for waking up people with a kiss."

"The women he wakes up tend to fall in love with him, too," Granny said. "It might be coincidence, but we'd rather not chance it."

"We don't want William Charming for a stepfather," Sabrina grumbled.

Uncle Jake crossed the room to Poppa Bear and patted his furry arm affectionately. "Good to see you again, old man. Your boy is getting big."

"You know the bears?" Goldilocks asked.

Uncle Jake nodded. "Oh, yes. Let's just say Poppa and Baby helped me retrieve a phantom scroll from a Romanian constable a few years back."

"Retrieve or steal, Jacob?" Goldilocks asked, raising her eyebrows.

Momma Bear growled. Sabrina didn't need to speak bear to hear her disapproval.

"To-may-toe, to-mah-toe," her uncle replied with a wink. "Goldie, we understand you and the bears have given up a lot in returning to Ferryport Landing. You're trapped here again, and we are very grateful for that sacrifice."

Poppa Bear gave a long bark.

"He says it was time to reunite his family," Goldilocks translated. "Momma Bear was the only one in the town when the barrier went up. They agreed it was best for Baby to live a life of freedom, but they've been apart too long. He says it's better to be trapped together than to be apart for another day."

"I don't mean to be rude," Sabrina interrupted. "But we've been waiting a long time for this to happen. Could we all catch up after we wake up Mom and Dad?"

"Of course," Goldilocks said. "So, Jake, you're the expert on magic. Do I just kiss Henry, and he'll wake up?"

"That's the word on the street," Uncle Jake said. "Briar Rose was under a similar spell, and she says there's no special trick to it. Just pucker up and lay one on him."

"Briar Rose said 'pucker up and lay one on him'?" Goldilocks asked.

"I'm paraphrasing," Uncle Jake said.

"This all depends on whether you still love my son," Granny said.

Goldie looked down at Henry and gave his hand a squeeze. "What about Veronica? I'm not going to be any help to her."

"Dad will take over once he's awake," Daphne reassured her.

Just then, the reflection in the mirror shimmered and shook. Its surface rippled like a bubbling brook, and when it finally calmed, an intimidating face materialized.

"WHO INVADES MY SANCTUARY?" it bellowed. Red yelped and tried to run, but Daphne held her hand tightly and promised that she was safe. Still, the girl shuddered with fear as she stared at the strange face floating in the glass.

"It's us, Mirror," Granny said. "No enemies here."

Mirror's features and voice brightened. "Am I missing something, Grimms?"

"Goldilocks has come back to smooch my dad," Daphne explained. "We think it will wake him up! Isn't that great news?"

"Great news, indeed." Mirror smiled. "Hello, Ms. G. It's nice to see your face in person again. We've been following your travels."

Goldilocks returned the smile. "It's good to see you, too, Mirror. Still looking great, I see."

Mirror smiled. "I owe it all to Pilates and vitamin C."

"Again, people, can we please get on with this?" Sabrina begged. All of this chitchat was excruciating. Her parents' curse had to be broken, immediately. She had waited so long for this moment. There had been many days when she had given up hope, convinced that her parents would sleep for all eternity. But, now, finally, her family would be reunited. Things would go back to normal. She was tired of waiting.

"OK, here goes," Goldilocks said. She tucked a curl behind her ear and leaned in close to Henry.

A loud fart from across the room stopped her in her tracks. Everyone turned in the direction of the horrible noise—and smell—to find Puck standing in the doorway. He was a shaggy-haired boy who, like Red, had been adopted by Granny Relda. Though he looked twelve, he was actually somewhere around four thousand years old. He wore pajamas and a long sleeping cap that dragged on the floor. He scratched his backside with a wooden sword and scowled.

"Can't a person get any sleep around here? I woke up because it sounded like there was a pack of bears running through the house, and look! There is! Are they moving in, too? Old lady, you've never met anyone you didn't hand a set of keys," Puck ranted. "I mean, after all, we've got a murderous lunatic who only wears one color."

"I'm sorry," Red Riding Hood squeaked.

Then Puck turned to Daphne. "A little monkey who eats us out of house and home."

"Hey!" Daphne protested.

Puck continued, turning to Sabrina. "And then there's this one. A girl so ugly that everyone stares and points at her. So why not some bears, too? Maybe we could invite a couple of giants while we're at it, or a bunch of those idiot Munchkins from across town. Why, you could even turn this place into a bed-and-breakfast for every Everafter who's down on their luck!"

"Well, someone woke up on the wrong side of the bed this morning." Uncle Jake chuckled.

"Puck, you're being rude," Granny said. "We're sorry we woke you, but Goldilocks has returned to help us wake up Henry and Veronica."

"Who?" the boy said.

"My parents, you moron!" Sabrina growled. "She's going to kiss my dad and break the magic spell. What did you think we've been trying to do for the past few months?!"

"Wait, these two are under a magic spell?" the boy asked. "I just thought they were really lazy. You can't expect me to know every little detail about what happens in this house."

He farted again, and this one was so loud that Elvis jumped and yelped in fear.

"Goldie, please, just kiss my dad already!" Sabrina begged.

Goldilocks nodded and leaned in once more. She hovered over Henry, her face just inches from his, and whispered something Sabrina couldn't hear. Then, she pressed her lips to his and closed her eyes.

Her kiss was gentle and a little longer than Sabrina would have liked. When she pulled away, Goldilocks's face was bright red. She looked as if she had been caught doing something illicit, but her expression was nothing compared to Uncle Jake's and Granny Relda's. They both looked utterly defeated.

"What? What's wrong?" Sabrina asked.

"It should have worked already," her uncle said.

"Try again," Granny urged.

Goldilocks squirmed. The first kiss had clearly been hard for her, and a second might break her heart. But, she kissed him again, anyway. Like the first kiss, this one seemed to have no effect on Henry's sleep.

"Perhaps Goldie isn't in love with Henry anymore," Mirror said. "It has been fifteen years since they were a couple. Sometimes, feelings fade."

Goldilocks said nothing but shook her head, her eyes fixed on the floor.

"Let's try one more time," Daphne said hopefully.

"It won't help," Uncle Jake said. "The spell is supposed to break immediately. He should be sitting up in bed already. This must be some new kind of sleeping spell we haven't encountered before. I'll call Briar and Snow. Maybe they will have some other ideas."

"So that's it? We're just giving up?" Sabrina cried, panicked.

"Of course we're not giving up," Uncle Jake said. "We're going back to the drawing board to find another solution."

Daphne flashed Sabrina a look that said "don't freak out," but it was way too late.

"This is a stupid wild-goose chase!" Sabrina exclaimed. "The Master and the Scarlet Hand are probably laughing at us right now!"

"Don't give up hope, Sabrina," Mirror said, reassuringly.

"Give up hope?! I haven't had any hope at all for two years." Bitter tears washed down Sabrina's cheeks. Why was the world so unfair? What had she done to deserve so much pain?

"Bummer," Puck said.

A faint knocking came from downstairs.

"Puck, could you please find out who is at the front door?" Granny asked.

"What am I? The butler?"

"I'll get it," Sabrina said. She needed to get out of the room. The disappointment was threatening to suffocate her.

"Whoever it is, don't forget to invite them to move in," Puck said sarcastically. "I'm sure the old lady will be happy to show them where we keep the towels!"

"Freaking out isn't going to help Mom and Dad," Daphne said as she raced down the stairs after Sabrina. "Everyone wanted this to work. Goldilocks gave up everything to try to help. Exploding in frustration every time we have a setback is—well, it's annoying."

Sabrina spun on her sister. "First of all, you don't even know the meaning of most of the words in that last sentence," she shouted. "Second, I have a right to be angry. This is the worst day of my life!"

Sabrina threw the door open to find a rail-thin woman with a hooked beak of a nose and eyes like tiny black holes. She was dressed entirely in gray. Her handbag was gray. Her hair was gray. When she smiled, even her teeth were gray.

"Ms. Smirt!" Sabrina gasped.

"Hello, girls," the woman said, coldly.

"I think it's about to get a lot worse," Daphne groaned.

"So nice to see that you remember me. It warms my heart." Ms. Smirt sneered as she snatched them by the wrists and dragged them outside. They were across the lawn and in a taxicab before either of them could fight back.

"Where are you taking us?" Daphne cried.

"Back to the orphanage," Smirt snapped. "Your grandmother is unfit to care for you. She kidnapped you from your foster father."

Sabrina remembered Mr. Greeley, a murderer with a criminal

record as long as her leg. "That foster father was a serial killer. He attacked us with a crowbar!"

"The father-child bond needs time to develop," Smirt said as she fastened seat belts across the girls' laps.

"You can't send us back to him," Daphne shouted. "He'll kill us!"

"And what a tragedy that would be for us all! It doesn't matter, anyway. Mr. Greeley is currently unavailable."

"So, he's back in jail?" Sabrina asked.

Smirt let out a telling "harrumph!"

"I've found you a new foster family. The father happens to be an amateur knife thrower. He's eager for some new targets—I mean, daughters," she said, then tossed a twenty-dollar bill at the driver. "You got automatic locks in this thing?"

Suddenly, Sabrina heard the cab's doors lock. She pulled at the handle, but it wouldn't budge.

"To the train station, please," she demanded. "And there's another twenty in it for you if we make the 8:14 to Grand Central."

Tires squealed as the taxi tore out of the driveway and made a beeline for the Ferryport Landing train station.

"You can't take us back to the orphanage," Sabrina said. "We're not orphans. We found our mother and father."

"Oh, yes, I forgot about your wild fantasy life, Sophie," Smirt said. "You know, there's really nothing more unattractive than a child with an imagination."

"My name is Sabrina!" she shrieked.

"Is it?" Smirt challenged with a smirk.

In record time, the taxi pulled into the station, where a train was waiting. With a firm pinch on the ear, Ms. Smirt hustled the girls aboard just as the doors were closing.

"Daphne, don't worry," Sabrina whispered to her sister. She had many talents, but her greatest was the ability to devise escape plans. She began studying the exit doors, windows, and even the emergency brake cable. A daring escape was already coming together when Daphne spoke up.

"I've got this one covered," she said.

"You what?" Sabrina asked.

The little girl put her palm into her mouth and bit down on it.

"What's going on, Daphne?" Sabrina pressed.

Her sister almost never plotted the escapes. Escaping was the exclusive domain of Sabrina Grimm. Was this another casualty of their strained relationship?

"Zip it!" Ms. Smirt snapped. "I don't want to sit on this train for two hours listening to a couple of chatterboxes." She reached into her handbag for a book and flipped it open.

"Ms. Smirt, have you ever heard of the Brothers Grimm?" Daphne asked.

The caseworker scowled and set her book on her lap. "What is this nonsense?"

"You've heard of the Brothers Grimm, right?"

"They wrote fairy tales," Ms. Smirt said, dismissing Daphne with a wave of her hand.

Daphne shook her head. "That's what most people think, but it's not true. The Brothers Grimm didn't write fictional stories; they recorded actual events. Their book is full of things that really happened. It's so the rest of us can learn about Everafters."

Sabrina was shocked. Daphne was spilling the family secret to the worst possible person. They couldn't trust Smirt any further than they could throw her.

"What's an Everafter?" the caseworker snapped.

"That's what fairy-tale characters like to be called," the little girl explained. "'Fairy-tale character' is kind of a rude term. It implies that they aren't real, and, like I was saying, the Brothers Grimm wrote about real events. Snow White is real. She ate a real poisoned apple. Cinderella, Prince Charming, Robin Hood—they're all real, and they live in Ferryport Landing. The Queen of Hearts is the mayor. Sleeping Beauty is dating our uncle."

Ms. Smirt peered closely at Daphne. "Debbie, I hope they make straitjackets in your size."

"It's Daphne," she corrected.

"Please be quiet," Sabrina whispered in her sister's ear.

"OK, kid, I'll bite. If fairy-tale characters are real, how come I haven't met any?" the caseworker asked.

"Because there's a magical wall that surrounds this town and keeps the Everafters locked inside. Wilhelm Grimm and a witch named Baba Yaga built it to stop any evil Everafters from invading nearby towns."

"Of course," Smirt said. She slapped her knee and let loose a loud, mocking cackle. "A magical wall!"

"They call it 'the barrier.' The Brothers Grimm are our ancestors, and because of what they did, a lot of Everafters don't like us," Daphne said. "But—"

"Daphne, stop. You've told her too much," Sabrina begged.

"Sabrina, I've got this," Daphne snapped, then turned her attention back to Smirt. "As I was saying, we have a few enemies in Ferryport Landing, but we've got a few friends, too."

Suddenly there was a tap on the window. Sabrina gazed out, expecting to see the Hudson River rushing past. Instead, she saw Puck. He was flying alongside the train, held aloft by his giant pink wings. He stuck his tongue out at her.

Ms. Smirt was horrified. She shrieked and tumbled onto the floor, scampering underneath her seat like a cockroach.

"Did you see that?" Ms. Smirt stammered. "There's a boy out there. Flying! Outside the window!"

Puck flew off, disappearing from view. A moment later, the ear-shattering screech of tearing metal filled the air. Something sailed past the window and splashed into the Hudson below. It looked like part of a train door.

"Did the two of you plan this?" Sabrina asked Daphne.

"Someone's got to think ahead in this family," she replied matter-of-factly.

Seconds later, Puck strolled down the aisle with his wings fully extended. "Well, well, well. Look at me, saving your butts, again. You know, you're kinda pathetic." He knelt down to peer at Smirt. The woman shrieked in terror and tried to scurry even farther under the seat.

"What is she doing down there?" he asked Sabrina.

"Hiding, I guess."

Puck leaned closer to Ms. Smirt and said, too loudly for the cramped space, "I found you! You're it!"

"Get him away from me!" Ms. Smirt whimpered.

Puck laughed and dragged the caseworker to her feet. Daphne stepped up to the trembling woman and patted her hand, gently. It did little to calm her. She was speechless. Her jaw fell open over and over, and she couldn't stop staring at Puck's wings.

"This is good-bye, Ms. Smirt," said Daphne.

"Wait! We can't go yet. We forgot the merciless kicking. That's my favorite part of the plan!" Puck said.

"I vetoed the kicking," Daphne said. "We're going to send Ms. Smirt back home unharmed."

Puck scowled. "Party pooper."

"What plan? What on earth is happening here?" Sabrina cried.

Before she could get an answer, the train conductor's voice came over the speaker system. "Next stop, Poughkeepsie!"

Daphne's face fell. "Uh-oh."

Puck blanched, and his mischievous grin vanished. "Uh-oh."

"Two 'uh-oh's? What's wrong?" Sabrina cried, panicking and spinning around in search of the threat. *What monster do we need to run from now?*

"The barrier!" Daphne shouted. "Puck! Run!"

Puck bolted, but it was too late. As the train passed through the invisible wall, he was knocked off his feet and sent sailing down the aisle.

"How do you stop this thing?" Puck cried, flailing helplessly as he was pushed along the train by the unseen magic.

Sabrina ran to the emergency brake cable and yanked it with all her might. The brakes screeched, and the train decelerated rapidly, causing suitcases and passengers alike to fly in every direction. Puck crashed into the steel door at the end of the car, knocking it off its hinges. His body kept skidding along the floor into the next car. He was going to crash into the next door but not with enough force to break through. The barrier would slowly crush him before the train completely stopped. Sabrina looked around frantically for something to use to smash the door open. But, when she looked back to Puck, the boy fairy had transformed into a full-size rhinoceros.

He lowered his head just as his diamond-hard horn plowed through the next train door.

"He turned into a rhino," Ms. Smirt said, finally regaining the ability to speak.

"Yeah, he does that," Daphne said, then grabbed Sabrina by the hand. "C'mon!"

The girls rushed after Puck, watching him blow through door after door and pushing past terrified commuters. Luckily, no one was injured, but many cowered behind copies of the *New York Times*, and Sabrina suspected that a few wet their pants.

When the trio reached the last car, Puck crashed through its door, tumbling out onto the tracks. The girls leaped to the ground after him. There was a crowd of people waiting to greet them.

Uncle Jake, Granny Relda, Elvis, Goldilocks, Red Riding Hood, and the three bears were all standing at the side of the tracks. Puck quickly morphed back into his true form, but Sabrina barely noticed. There were two people waiting there who made her wonder if she was hallucinating. She blinked a few times and then looked to her grandmother, who was grinning widely.

Henry and Veronica Grimm, her parents, waited with out-stretched arms.

"Mom? Dad?" she cried.

Henry and Veronica rushed to the girls and scooped them up. Veronica peppered Sabrina and Daphne with kisses. Henry squeezed so hard, Sabrina could barely breathe. She loved every second of it.

"Girls," their father choked. "My dear, sweet girls."

"But I thought our plan didn't work," Daphne said.

"It must have worked!" Henry said.

"You know your father. He loves to sleep late," Veronica explained.

Henry and Veronica stepped back to study their daughters. "Girls, you look so different," her father said.

Veronica held Daphne's face in her hand. "You're so . . . big."

"You've been asleep a really long time," Daphne said.

Henry turned to Granny Relda with questioning eyes.

"How long?" he asked.

"Nearly two years," the old woman said, sadly.

"Two years!" Veronica cried.

Sabrina's parents looked as if someone had punched them in the gut, the shock clear on their faces. "Th-that can't be true," Henry stammered.

"I'm afraid it is," Uncle Jake said.

Henry turned to Goldilocks. "What are you doing here?" he asked.

"There's a lot to tell you," Granny Relda said.

"But what's important is we're together now," Sabrina said brightly, trying to shift everyone's attention back to the happy reunion. All the worries that had haunted her over the last two years evaporated. The incredible weight of being responsible for herself and Daphne lifted from her shoulders, and for the first time in years she felt like a kid.

Just in time to ruin Sabrina's happy moment, Ms. Smirt scurried through the busted train door. She smoothed her gray suit and struggled with a broken heel on one of her shoes. She straightened, as if mustering all of her strength. "These children are wards of the state, and they're coming with me, flying boy or no flying boy."

"Who is this woman?" Henry asked.

"She's our caseworker," Sabrina explained. "When you vanished, we were sent to live in an orphanage. She placed us with foster parents."

"Horrible, evil foster parents," Daphne said. "She sent us to live with a man who was terrified of soap!"

"Don't forget the family with the Bengal tiger living in their house!" Sabrina said.

"And the guy who had us collect roadkill for his restaurant!"

Veronica grabbed Smirt by the collar. "Have you been mistreating my children?"

"I did what was in the best interests of your brood," Smirt sneered as she tried to break free.

"I think that what's in the best interest of my 'brood' is for them to watch me knock you out," Veronica said.

"Are you threatening me?" the caseworker gasped.

"Of course I am," Veronica replied.

Smirt finally broke free and scampered back up onto the train.

"We can't let her go. She knows everything. She'll go back to the city and tell everyone what she's learned," Sabrina said.

"Exactly." Daphne grinned. "They'll think she's a nutcase. They'll either fire her or give her a straitjacket of her own."

Sabrina was astounded. Daphne's idea was genius. It finally rid them of Smirt and the orphanage forever. Actually, the little girl's plan was even better than anything Sabrina would have dreamed up.

"OK, but we should probably put some forgetful dust on the other passengers," Granny Relda suggested. "I suspect seeing a rhino on their morning commute has given them a serious case of the frights."

"You can't erase it from their brains! Freaking people out is my art, and I just created a masterpiece, old lady!" Puck protested.

"I'm afraid we have no choice, *liebling*," Granny Relda said. "And when we're finished, we'll need to hurry home. There is so much to tell Henry and Veronica."

"Forget it, Mom," Henry said, taking his girls' hands in his own. "We're leaving as soon as the girls are packed."

"Leaving?" Granny cried.

Sabrina and Daphne eyed one another in astonishment.

Henry nodded. "Yes. We're getting out of Ferryport Landing as fast as we can."

2

B IG BROTHER, THIS IS NOT ONE OF YOUR BEST ideas," Jake said. "You've been missing for two years—do you realize what that means? Most people think you and Veronica are dead. Your apartment has been sold. There's mountains of paperwork you'd need to do before you can get any of your money. Neither one of you has a job, and if you're smart, you'll steer clear of that caseworker and the board of child welfare. There's so much to sort out, and we can help."

"He makes some good points, Henry," Veronica said. "Maybe we should stay put until we get everything settled."

Sabrina's father shook his head stubbornly. "Getting out of Ferryport Landing is more important than any of those inconveniences."

Granny Relda looked to be on the verge of tears. Sabrina had never seen her so upset. "But, Henry—"

"It's not open for discussion, Mom," he snapped.

Veronica frowned but held her tongue.

"I don't think you'll be able to get to Manhattan until the train gets cleaned up," Goldilocks said, gesturing to the mess still on the tracks.

"Fine," Henry growled, and then marched up the embankment to the parking lot. The group followed in tense silence. Soon, they found the family's ancient car. Oil leaked onto the asphalt, and a mysterious green fluid seeped from the muffler.

"I can't believe you still drive this hunk of junk, Jake," Veronica said.

"She's family," Jake said. "You can't abandon family."

Henry's face went red. A fight was on the horizon.

This day was not turning out the way Sabrina had dreamed. "How did you get everyone into the car?" she asked, hoping to change the subject. "You couldn't fit the bears inside even if you squeezed."

"That was my doing," Uncle Jake said with a wink. He reached into one of his jacket pockets and took out a small wooden box. Inside was a green dust that spun around in a tiny tornado.

Daphne's eyes lit up with wonder. "What's that?"

"One of the few magical items I have left after Baba Yaga stole my other coat. It's stretching powder. I got it from the little old lady who lives in a shoe. With seventy rug rats in one old boot, she had to get creative."

"How does it work?" Daphne asked.

"You can make something as big or as small as you want for a limited amount of time with just a sprinkle. I blew a handful into the car, and now it's big enough for a whole forest of bears."

"So gravy!" Daphne said, eyeing the green particles.

"Gravy?" Sabrina asked. The little girl was always coming up with silly new phrases or words.

Daphne ignored her sister and kept her attention on Uncle Jake. "Can I try?"

Henry snatched the box, snapped it shut, and stuffed it into one of Jake's pockets. "Keep your magic away from the girls," he growled. "It's dangerous, and I don't want them anywhere near it."

"Dad, don't worry," Daphne said. "We use magic all the time."

Henry glared at his mother. It was obvious he didn't approve.

"I'm getting pretty good, too," Daphne continued, completely oblivious to her father's rising temper. "In fact, I have a few wands and an enchanted ring of my own, just like a real witch."

"A five-year-old shouldn't be within a hundred miles of magic!" Henry cried. "Hand everything over to me as soon as we get to the house. None of that nonsense is going back to New York City."

"Dad, I'm not five years old. I'll be eight in two weeks," Daphne said.

Henry froze and gaped at his daughter as if she were speaking ancient Greek.

"Maybe we should go," Goldilocks said with a forced smile. She opened one of the rusty car doors and helped the bears lumber into the backseat.

Sabrina and Daphne followed and couldn't help but marvel at what they found. Uncle Jake's stretching powder did the trick: The car's interior was enormous, even bigger than Granny Relda's living room.

Veronica took a seat between her daughters and wrapped an arm around each of them. "So, what have we missed?"

"Granny's been teaching us to be detectives," Daphne said, excitedly.

Granny shifted uncomfortably.

"You knew I didn't want them involved in the family business," Henry interrupted.

"We've been careful. They've both been perfectly safe," Granny said.

Sabrina laughed, and the entire family turned to face her.

"You disagree?" Henry asked her.

Sabrina felt Granny's betrayed eyes on her. "No," she mumbled.

"Sabrina, if you have something to say, I'd like to hear it," Henry demanded.

"It was nothing, really. Just a giant attack, and then Rumpelstiltskin was eating my emotions, and then we killed the Jabberwocky, and—"

"It's dead?" Henry asked, bewildered.

Granny Relda nodded.

"What else, Sabrina?" her father pressed.

"I was turned into a frog and almost eaten by Baba Yaga, we were attacked by a giant robot, nearly killed by Titania, sucked into a time vortex—"

"Time vortex?" cried Veronica.

"It was so cool, Mom," Daphne said. "We met our future selves. Sabrina was married!"

"Daphne!" Sabrina screeched. No one knew the complete truth about what the girls had seen in the future. Her marriage and, most importantly, the identity of her husband, were supposed to be kept secret. If Puck ever found out . . .

"Married?" Puck laughed. "Who would marry you? He must be blind."

Sabrina clenched her fists. She had no idea what her older self saw in the smelly, annoying fairy. She had to admit that Puck's grown-up version was very cute, but how had she gotten over all the insults, pranks, and mean-spirited jokes? Maybe there weren't any other men in the future? That could be the only explanation.

"Anything else?" Henry demanded.

"Yeah, we were barbecued by dragons, Sabrina was taken over by the rabid spirit of the Big Bad Wolf, and . . . I think that covers it," Daphne finished.

"We had a yard sale, too," Uncle Jake said from his place in the driver's seat.

"Go ahead, Jake. Make a joke out of it like you always do," Henry said.

"Relax, Hank. Mom protected them every step of the way. I've been here for most of it, too," Jake said.

Elvis let out a low growl.

"The dog wants to remind everyone of his contributions," Goldilocks said.

Daphne hugged the big dog. "We all know you're the real hero, Elvis."

Elvis barked.

"He says heroes deserve sausages," Goldilocks translated.

"And what about me?" Puck said. "I've been pulling this family from the jaws of death on a daily basis and haven't seen a dime for my troubles."

Henry scowled. "If you don't mind, we're having a family discussion. Who are you, anyway? Peter Pan?"

"Henry!" Granny cried. "No! He's very sensitive about—"

"I AM NOT PETER PAN!" Puck bellowed as smoke blasted out of his nose and mouth. In his outburst, he blew the top of the family car into the air, turning the old jalopy into a very crude convertible.

No one was hurt, but the family launched into a massive, many-sided argument. Granny argued with Veronica. Henry shouted at Puck. The three bears roared and snapped at one another. All Sabrina could do was watch quietly and hope no one turned on her.

When a little hand slipped into hers and gave it a quick squeeze, Sabrina was elated that Daphne had finally turned to her. But, when she looked down, she found Red Riding Hood. The little girl trembled in fright, unnerved by all the shouting.

Sabrina couldn't bring herself to comfort Red. She yanked her hand away as if it had slipped into the mouth of an alligator. Red seemed hurt but didn't say a word.

Finally, Granny Relda put her fingers in her mouth and blasted a high-pitched, ear-rattling whistle. Everyone fell silent, and she turned her attention to Uncle Jake.

"Jacob, why in heaven's name are you driving so fast?"

Sabrina eyed the speedometer. The red needle was pushing one hundred and ten.

"Because we have a major problem!" Jake cried.

"What are you talking about?" Henry asked.

"Well, big brother, when you insulted Puck, he blew the roof off the car, and now the integrity of the interior is compromised," he shouted over the wind.

"In English, please," Veronica said.

"I enchanted the inside of the car to fit all of you in it. Now, the inside is also the outside," Jake explained.

"So?" Granny asked.

"So, now the magic has two choices. It can make the whole world bigger, which would be very, very bad. I'm talking earthquakes, tsunamis, all kinds of insane weather. Real. Bad. Stuff."

"And what's the other choice?" Goldilocks asked.

"The interior of the car is going to shrink back to its normal size," Jake explained. "Which means it's going to get very cramped back there very fast."

Sabrina looked to the three bears. Each probably weighed around eight hundred pounds. "How fast?"

She heard a popping sound, followed by a loud hiss. As the car rapidly shrunk, she was pushed roughly to the center of the backseat until she was nearly on her mother's lap.

"Drive faster!" Henry shouted over the wind that beat against his face.

"Don't tell me what to do," Uncle Jake said.

"Then don't drive like an old woman!" Henry snapped.

"They sound like you two," Puck said to Sabrina and Daphne. Both girls glared at him.

The faster Jake drove, the quicker the car seemed to shrink. Sabrina soon found Puck's nose within an inch of her own. If the backseat got much tighter, they would be pushed even closer together. Accidents could happen! Accidents with lips!

"I hope you brushed this morning," Puck said, closing his eyes and puckering up for a kiss.

"Uncle Jake, drive faster!" Sabrina begged.

"Fine! I don't want to kiss you, anyway. I'm out of here," Puck snarled. His wings unfurled, and he leaped into the air, flying high above the car. Sabrina was relieved, but not for long. When the car shrank again, her face was forced into Poppa Bear's hairy armpit.

When they finally arrived at the house, Uncle Jake pulled into the front yard, barreling through shrubbery and bringing the car to a halt just inches from the porch. Everyone spilled out of the car and onto the lawn. Baby Bear toppled over Goldilocks. Elvis jumped out and scurried under a bush. When Uncle Jake opened his door, he fell out along with Veronica and Granny Relda. Sabrina hit the ground with a thud, then looked for her sister. Daphne was nowhere to be seen.

"Daphne!" she cried. "Did she fall out?"

Momma Bear grunted and got up from her seat. There, beneath her, was Daphne—a little mushed, but safe.

"I have never needed a bath so much in my entire life," the little girl groaned.

"Do you see now, Jake? This is exactly what I'm talking about. We all could have been hurt by that magic," Henry said. "Veronica, take the girls inside and help them pack. Don't let them bring anything that can cast a spell."

"Henry, really—" Granny Relda started.

He cut her off. "Mom, I need to use your phone. I'm going to call everyone we know in New York City. Someone will take us in, at least for a few nights." He turned to Sabrina and Daphne. "Go on, girls. Go with your mother."

Granny unlocked the front door, and the girls climbed the stairs with their mother. In their bedroom, Veronica slumped down on the bed, clearly drained. Tears began to stream down her face.

"Don't cry," Sabrina said, wrapping her mother in a hug. "We're all together now."

"I can't believe how long we've been apart. You must have been so frightened." Veronica cupped Sabrina's face in her hands. "You did a good job looking after your sister."

Sabrina's belly filled up with a million happy butterflies. Her mother's approval was like a lifetime of birthday presents rolled into one.

"And you've both gotten so pretty," Veronica continued. "My little girls—where did they go?"

"We're still here," Daphne said. "We're just bigger versions."

Veronica laughed.

"Mom, you have to talk to Dad. We can't go back to the city now," Daphne said, her tone suddenly serious. "We're needed here in Ferryport Landing."

"'Needed'?" Veronica replied.

"Absolutely! There's a lot of crazy shenanigans going on in this town, and Granny needs help keeping the peace," the little girl explained. "There's a bunch of bad guys called the Scarlet Hand running around tormenting everyone, and it seems like every time we turn around, someone is on the verge of destroying the world. We can't leave."

"Daphne, you need to understand your father's point of view. This place holds a lot of bad memories for him. His father died here. I don't love the idea of going back to the city unprepared either, but we can't stay here. I think we should start packing."

Sabrina dutifully pulled two tiny suitcases out from under the bed. They were the same ones she and her sister had brought when they arrived in Ferryport Landing.

"Happy?" Daphne asked.

"Daphne, I—"

"You've hated being here since the first day. Well, you finally got what you wanted."

"That's not fair," Sabrina said.

"Girls, please don't fight," Veronica begged.

"I don't want to go," Daphne said. "Granny Relda has been training us to be detectives. That's what I want to do. She needs our help. And I can't just abandon Elvis and Puck, either."

"Daphne, your father has very strong feelings about this town. I'm not any happier about this than you are. I'll try to talk to him, but I can't promise he'll change his mind. If you're passionate about being a fairy-tale detective, there's plenty of work to do back home in the city."

"Mom, we already know all about the stuff you do behind

Dad's back. We've been to the fairy kingdom. Oz tried to kill us, and Sabrina was possessed by a ghost at Scrooge's accounting office. We even fought pirates on the Staten Island Ferry."

Veronica cringed. "That was supposed to be a secret."

Henry appeared in the doorway. "What's supposed to be a secret?" His eyes darted from Veronica to Daphne and finally to Sabrina. He raised his eyebrows at her as if he was sure she'd spill the beans. It made her feel ashamed.

"It's nothing," Veronica said. "Henry, the girls have a lot of things. Packing them might take a while."

"There's a train in half an hour, and I want to be on it. Pack what you can. We can send for the rest later."

"Are you really thinking this through?" she asked.

Henry scowled. "Don't fight with me, Veronica. Not about this."

Sabrina was surprised by her father's tone. He had always been so easygoing and carefree. Now, he was furious, his face so red and hot, she was sure she could fry an egg on it. A moment later, he stormed out of the room, shouting for his mother as he stomped down the stairs.

"You heard him," Veronica whispered.

The girls packed what they could in the space of a few minutes and brought their suitcases out into the hallway.

"I'd like to say good-bye to Mirror," Sabrina said.

"C'mon!" her father raged from downstairs.

"There's no time," Veronica said. "Mirror will understand."

Granny Relda and Uncle Jake waited by the door. Henry was pacing the foyer. Puck was lounging on the couch using his belly as a conga drum. Red Riding Hood sat in a dark corner. The three bears huddled around the dining room table, munching on a huge watermelon. Goldilocks was rearranging the rest of the bookshelves, and Elvis was lying on the floor, moaning sadly.

"Where are you going to go?" Granny Relda asked.

"Don't worry, Mom. We'll be fine," Henry said. "Jake, can you give us a ride to the train station, or should I call a taxi?"

"Henry, be reasonable. You can stay here until you get on your feet," Uncle Jake pleaded.

Henry shook his head. "We're going, Jake."

Granny extended her arms to the girls for a hug. They hugged her with all their might. "*Lieblings*, my heart will be empty until I see you again. Look after yourselves, and try not to bicker. You make a great team when you put your heads together."

Daphne sobbed as she leaned down and kissed Elvis on the snout. He barked.

"He says he doesn't want you to go," Goldilocks translated.

"I don't want to go," Daphne said.

Puck stopped his drumming. "What's going on?"

"We're moving back to Manhattan," Sabrina explained.

Puck sat up and stared at her. She expected a dismissive joke or some mean-spirited insult, but instead he looked confused, even troubled. "Really?"

Henry took his daughters' suitcases and marched outside. The girls reluctantly followed, but they were stopped in their tracks by a mob of people surrounding the house. The crowd was made up of Everafters of all stripes: cyclopes, ogres, stone golems, witches, warlocks, toy soldiers, trolls, and more.

At the front of the crowd was Mayor Heart, also known as the Queen of Hearts from *Alice's Adventures in Wonderland*. She wore a gaudy red dress and brandished an electronic megaphone. Standing next to her was the Sheriff of Nottingham, dressed from head to toe in leather, complete with boots, gloves, and a cape. A crossbow was flung across his back, and a dagger hung at his waist. A grotesque purple scar ran from the tip of his eye to the corner of his mouth. On his chest was a familiar, frightening symbol: a bloodred handprint. Each member of the crowd sported the same mark.

"Well, as I live and breathe, Henry Grimm is here. How was your nap?" the mayor cackled.

"Mrs. Heart, I'm taking my girls and leaving town. We aren't looking for any trouble," Henry said.

The mayor spoke into her megaphone. "Well, Henry, it appears trouble came looking for you."

Granny stepped forward. "Now, you listen to me—"

"NO!" the mayor bellowed. The megaphone emitted an ear-shattering feedback whine. "*You* listen to *me*! No one is going anywhere until you tell me what the Master wants to know."

"What are you talking about?" Uncle Jake asked.

"Where are Charming and the Wolf? We know they have fled into the forest, along with Robin Hood and his gang. Where are they hiding?"

"Like we'd tell you!" Daphne snarled.

Nottingham slid a silver arrow into his crossbow and aimed it at the little girl. "Tell us where their camp is, and I'll let you live through the day. As for tomorrow—no promises."

Uncle Jake stepped in front of Daphne. "Sheriff, every time your stupid little group threatens us, we make you look like fools. Why don't you save yourself the humiliation and get off our lawn before I—"

A whizzing sound filled the air, and then Uncle Jake let out a sharp cry. He fell, an arrow lodged deeply in his right shoulder. Blood leaked through his shirt and onto the porch.

"Perhaps you didn't hear the mayor," Nottingham snarled as he loaded his weapon with a fresh arrow. "Tell us where they are now!"

"Girls, get into the house!" Henry commanded. He caught Sabrina and Daphne by their shoulders and pushed them through the doorway.

Veronica and Granny Relda followed the girls, and Henry dragged his brother to safety. Once everyone was inside, he slammed the door just in time to block another of Nottingham's arrows.

"House, time to lock up!" Granny shouted with a sharp knock on the door. "OK, everyone, stay calm. We'll be safe in here," Granny reassured her family as she bent to tend to her wounded son. "Daphne, run upstairs and grab a bottle of iodine out of the medicine cabinet. It's a red bottle. Sabrina and Puck, go to the laundry room and get some sheets out of the dryer. Rip them into bandages. Goldilocks and Red, can you boil a pot of water?"

Everyone leaped into action, except Sabrina, who was frozen in shock.

"Sabrina! Go!" Granny shouted.

Sabrina snapped out of it, racing after Puck into the laundry room. She opened the dryer door and pulled out a fresh, clean sheet. Puck tore it apart with zeal.

"I didn't see that coming at all!" Puck said, excitedly.

"You sound like you're proud of the sheriff or something," Sabrina grumbled.

"Only professionally. As a villain, I can appreciate that he has stepped up his game," the fairy boy replied. "Still, that getup he wears is ridiculous. A leather cape is way over the top."

"There's no time for jokes, Puck," she groaned as they raced back to Uncle Jake's side. Goldilocks had returned with the hot water and

Daphne with the iodine. Everyone else seemed to be in a heated argument, and—once again—her father was at the center.

"This is exactly why we're going back to New York City," he snapped, as he pressed his hand firmly against his brother's wound. Nottingham's arrow was still protruding from Jake's shoulder.

"Henry, not now," Veronica begged.

"If the rest of you were smart, you'd come with us," Henry said, ignoring his wife.

"And let those maniacs out of the town?" Uncle Jake challenged through gritted teeth. "If we leave, the barrier falls, and they all go free. But I don't want to argue right now. I just want this arrow out."

Goldilocks herded the children together. "All right, kids, I need your help in the kitchen."

Puck stubbornly stomped his foot. "No way! I want to see this. I've shot a few arrows at people in my day, but I've never seen any of them come out. This is the opportunity of a lifetime!"

"Suit yourself," Goldilocks said, and she hurried Sabrina, Daphne, Red, and Baby Bear into the kitchen. Once there, she nervously searched the cabinets and refrigerator.

"What are you looking for?" Sabrina asked.

"Cocoa," the woman said. "Everything is better with some hot cocoa. Oh, these cabinets. How do you find anything in here?"

Daphne pointed Goldilocks in the right direction. Sabrina pulled the milk from the fridge, and Goldilocks put it on the stove to heat.

"Why are those mean people attacking us?" Red asked.

"They don't like us very much," Sabrina replied.

Baby Bear growled.

"Junior wants to know why someone doesn't just tell them where Charming and Mr. Canis have gone," Goldilocks said.

"Well, first of all, we don't know," Daphne explained. "And, second of all, even if we did, we wouldn't betray them. They're our friends."

Uncle Jake's horrible cry came from the living room. Daphne's face went white.

"I guess they got the arrow out," Sabrina said with a grimace.

"He'll be fine, kids," Goldilocks assured them as she rearranged the silverware in the drawers.

Puck rushed into the kitchen looking exhilarated, as if he had just gotten off a roller coaster. "That was awesome!" he crowed. "I think the arrow going in is more fun to watch, but that was still pretty cool."

"You're a troubling little boy," Goldilocks said to him.

He smiled so wide it was a wonder his face didn't permanently stretch. "Thanks. That's very nice of you to say."

Henry and Granny Relda hurried into the kitchen.

"We need to get Jake to a hospital," Henry said. "That's an open wound. He's going to need stitches and antibiotics. It could get infected if it's not cared for properly."

Granny Relda shook her head. "The hospital is deserted. All the doctors were human, and Mayor Heart ran them out of town."

"There has to be someone here with some medical training. Can Doctor Dolittle help?" Henry said, taking a glass from the cupboard.

"I think he's part of the Scarlet Hand," Granny said.

Henry turned the faucet on, but only a couple of brown drops trickled out. "They've turned off the pipes."

Suddenly, the lights went out.

"And the lights," Sabrina added.

"So we can't watch the television? This is war!" Puck cried. "I'm going upstairs to get my sword. You don't mess with the television!"

"I don't think fighting our way out is the answer, Puck," Granny said.

"Maybe not *the* answer but certainly *an* answer," Puck grumbled.

"Let's go ask the man with all the answers," Granny said. She led everyone back through the living room. Jake's shoulder was wrapped in bandages, and he was unconscious.

"He fainted from the pain," Veronica explained.

Henry heaved his brother onto Poppa Bear's back, and the group marched up the stairs to Mirror's room.

"WHO DARES . . . oh, it's you," Mirror said, and the flames vanished. "This place is starting to get as busy as Grand Central Station, Relda."

"This isn't even half of the guests," Granny Relda said. "The Scarlet Hand has surrounded the house."

"And Jake!" Mirror cried, noticing his state. "He's been injured!"

"Quite seriously, I'm afraid. We need to get him to a doctor, right away," Henry said. "We need the slippers."

"Which slippers are you referring to, Hank?"

"Dorothy's slippers," Henry said, impatiently. "We'll use them to teleport out of the house."

"Sorry, Hankster," Mirror said. "I lent them to your daughters awhile back, and one of them was lost."

"You lost Dorothy's slippers?" Henry cried, glaring at the girls.

"A giant was chasing us," Sabrina said defensively.

"A really big giant," Daphne added.

"Fine. We'll take the Gnome King's belt, instead," Henry said, turning his attention back to Mirror. "It does the same thing."

Mirror shook his head. "The girls ran down the batteries. If you have forty-six size Ds, then we're back in business."

Henry sighed. "For once, I'm turning to magic to solve a problem, and there's nothing available?! What have we got that will zap us out of this house?"

"We're a little short on zapping," Granny Relda explained. "But, there is still a way out of the house."

"There is?" Sabrina and Daphne asked.

Granny produced her set of keys. "Yes. There's a back door in the Room of Reflections."

"The what?" Red asked.

"You'll see," the old woman said.

Granny stepped through the mirror and vanished. Henry and Veronica followed, then Red, Daphne, Sabrina, and Puck. Elvis bounded through next. The three bears growled nervously, but Goldilocks huffed something back that seemed to calm them down. A moment later, they followed, Poppa Bear carrying Uncle Jake through to the other side.

The vastness of the Hall of Wonders never ceased to amaze Sabrina. Marble columns taller and thicker than redwood trees held the ceiling aloft. The hallway itself seemed to go on forever. Both sides held hundreds of doors made from a limitless variety of materials: wood, steel, stone, crystal. There was one door made from something Granny called protoplasm. All of the doors were labeled with brass plaques that explained the contents of their rooms.

"How come we've never heard of this Room of Reflections?" Daphne asked her grandmother.

"We don't use it very often, and it's not exactly within walking distance," the old woman replied. "It's all the way at the other end of the hall."

This piqued Sabrina's curiosity. She often wondered what was at the end of the Hall of Wonders.

Granny handed Mirror her set of keys. "We're going to need the trolley."

"Costume change!" Mirror cried, then stepped through a set of double doors to his immediate right. A moment later, Sabrina heard a bell ring, and then an old-fashioned trolley car plowed through the doors and stopped in front of the group. Mirror sat in the driver's seat, wearing a short green jacket, a black cap, and a money changer attached to his belt. He rang a polished brass bell and shouted, "All aboard!"

The girls climbed up while Henry helped Uncle Jake and the others get settled. Once everyone was aboard, Mirror rang the bell one final time and shouted, "Next stop, the Room of Reflections!" He shifted a lever, and the trolley lurched forward, rapidly gaining speed.

"I've always wanted to know what was at the end of the hall," Daphne said.

"Me too," Henry admitted.

"You've never seen it?" Sabrina asked, surprised.

"Jake and I tried to walk it once, back before we got the trolley.

We brought a tent and everything, but we forgot to pack food. After a day of walking we had to turn around and go back."

Mirror turned in his seat. "Folks, I'm going to put the pedal to the metal, as they say. So keep your hands and feet inside the vehicle at all times, and please, hold on tight."

Everything around Sabrina turned into a blur of color and light as the trolley sped to an impossible pace. The engine screamed, as did a few of the passengers. It was terrifying. Puck, however, seemed to be having the time of his life.

"Faster!" he begged. "It's not fun until someone wets their pants!"

Just a minute later, the trolley slowed, and the world came back into focus. Sabrina stepped off feeling light-headed and a little sick. She held on to the side of the trolley for balance. It seemed that everyone else in the group felt just as woozy, except for Puck, who begged Mirror for another ride. Once Sabrina felt better, she peered around the unfamiliar length of the Hall of Wonders.

The doors at this end were even more bizarre than the ones she already knew. One was made of a whirling blue gas with ancient skeletons suspended in it. Another was like the mouth of a huge monster, with sharp teeth and a horrible forked tongue. Another door was constructed from the gigantic bones of some prehistoric animal. There was also a more ordinary wooden door, with two stones recessed in the wood. Each of the stones had a handprint engraved in it, but the brass plaque for this door was not labeled.

"That's weird," Sabrina muttered to herself.

To the left was a massive wall, much like the one at their end of the hall. This one, however, didn't have a magical portal, only a single door made from rough stone. Intricate symbols that looked like hieroglyphics were chiseled into its surface. Sabrina had no idea what any of it meant, but the biggest of the symbols gave her a creepy feeling. It was a large sculpted eye. It moved like a real eye and studied each person in turn.

"Creepy!" Daphne squirmed as she watched its gaze move up and down the length of her body.

The most interesting difference between this door and all of the others was that it didn't have a lock. All of the doors in the Hall of Wonders were locked tight except for this one, which opened easily when Mirror pushed it. Inside, the group found a circular room draped in black curtains. Lining the walls were twenty-five full-length mirrors, each an equal distance apart. Sabrina suddenly understood why Granny called it the Room of Reflections.

"Are these magic mirrors?" Veronica asked, running her hand along one's surface. The tips of her fingers disappeared into the glass, and the image rippled like the surface of a pond.

"Not exactly," Mirror explained. "They're actually the back doors to every magic mirror the Wicked Queen created."

"Are you saying that we can step through these and come out into another Hall of Wonders?" Goldilocks asked.

Mirror looked slightly offended. "My dear, there is only one Hall of Wonders and only one me. Each of the mirrors my mother created is unique, and each mirror comes equipped with its own unique guardian."

"Like Harry from the Hotel of Wonders," Daphne said.

"Harry?" her father asked.

"Mr. Charming has a magic mirror," Daphne explained. "It has a hotel inside it, run by Harry. He's really nice."

"There will be plenty of time to talk about the mirrors once Jake is in good hands," Granny Relda said. "For now, we're going to step through one of them and use it to go to the real world, hopefully, far away from the mob outside."

"An excellent idea," Mirror said, and then puffed up his chest with pride. "My mother designed me to be the hub, a gateway to the other mirrors, making me all the more unique."

"Gravy!" Daphne cried as she rushed to the closest mirror. "Let's use this one!"

Before she could jump into the reflection, Granny Relda snatched her arm and yanked her back. "*Liebling*, no!" She pointed to a sign hanging at the bottom of the mirror that read OUT OF SERVICE. "You can't just jump into these things. Some of them don't work correctly."

"She's right," Mirror said, pointing to a few others with the same sign. "Thirteen of the mirrors have, unfortunately, been broken beyond repair. Two more are buried beneath the earth, and who knows what's crawled into them. Another is filled with a poisonous gas, and yet another is, from what I can tell, at the bottom of the Atlantic Ocean. Two others have been shattered and their guardians destroyed. If you were to step into one of them, you would be cut to ribbons. In my free time I've been removing the shards from the frames."

He gestured to a pile of broken glass on the floor.

Sabrina did the math in her head. "That leaves six magic mirrors that are still working."

"Do you think one of these will lead us to a doctor?" Henry asked impatiently.

"If we pick the right one," Granny said as she turned to Sabrina and Daphne. "That's where you two come in."

"Us?"

"Yes. I think it would be unwise to just step into any one of these mirrors, especially since we don't know what kind of guardian might be inside or where they might lead. You two, however, have been inside one and know the guardian quite well. You say his name is Harry? Do you think you can find him?"

"Sure," Daphne said.

The girls went from one portal to the next, skipping the broken ones. One reflected nothing back at them, but all of the others showed something entirely unique. One revealed a medieval torture chamber. Another mirror looked into an old-fashioned ice-cream parlor, and yet another revealed a huge warehouse filled with thousands of crates and boxes. In one, Sabrina saw a tacky nightclub with a disco ball and strobe lights.

"Here it is," Daphne cried from across the room.

Sabrina rushed over and peered into the mirror to find a breath-taking sunset. Swaying palm trees and a sandy beach invited them to enter.

"Not so fast, girls," Henry said, stepping toward the mirror. "I'll go first."

"Dad, it's perfectly safe," Daphne said.

He ignored her. It was the second time he had totally dismissed her opinion, and Sabrina noticed her sister's frustration building. Sabrina had learned the hard way to take Daphne seriously. It looked like her father had some lessons of his own to learn.

Henry took a tentative step into the mirror, dipping his head inside to take a look around. A moment later he reappeared. "Coast is clear, folks. Let's hurry." He waved them through.

Sabrina found herself once again standing at the front desk of an incredibly swanky hotel. The floor was polished marble with beautiful Persian rugs scattered about. The walls were adorned with tasteful contemporary masterpieces. Everything sparkled under the grand crystal chandelier, and a bank of floor-to-ceiling windows revealed a tropical paradise pretty enough for a postcard.

Harry appeared from behind the front desk. He was a short Asian man wearing a Hawaiian shirt with a stack of leis in his arms. He placed one around everybody's neck as he welcomed them enthusiastically. When he got to the bears, he discovered he wasn't tall enough to reach over their heads, so he simply placed a lei into each of their paws. Poppa Bear promptly ate his.

"Aloha!" Harry cried. "Sabrina! Daphne! Welcome back to the Hotel of Wonders. Are you here on business or pleasure?"

"Neither," Sabrina replied. "In fact, we're just passing through. We've got an emergency on our hands."

"From what I understand, you and your family find yourselves in emergencies quite frequently," Harry said with a knowing grin. "How can I help?"

"We want to use your portal to get to the real world," Henry said impatiently.

"Oh, so you slipped in the back way. This way to the portal," Harry announced, escorting everyone through the hotel lobby. "The boss has been here a lot lately. He's pretty busy with his camp. I'm not sure why he doesn't open some rooms to the refugees. We have plenty of space."

"Knowing him, he probably doesn't want the riffraff ruining the sheets," Sabrina commented.

"What does *riffraff* mean?" Daphne asked.

Sabrina automatically opened her mouth to explain but then remembered the girl's reaction the last time she'd tried to define a word. She decided to let someone else play dictionary for a change.

"*Riffraff* is a mean word rich people use to describe poor people," Veronica said.

"Harry, did you say Charming is working with refugees?" Goldilocks asked.

"Yes, there were quite a number of citizens in Ferryport Landing who refused to join the Scarlet Hand. Heart and the others ran them from their homes, so the boss has offered them sanctuary in his camp. I hear there's a fairly large population."

"Wait a minute!" Henry cried. "Your portal leads us to his camp? Mom, that won't work. We need to go back and pick a different mirror."

"Heavens, why?" the old woman asked.

"Have you forgotten? He threatened to destroy our family! He said he was going to bulldoze our house!"

"Billy has changed since you knew him," Granny said as she wiped Uncle Jake's brow with a damp cloth. "Now he's the closest thing we have to an ally in the Everafter community. If Mr. Canis has learned to trust him, so can you."

"Mr. Canis is at the camp, too?" Red whimpered.

Granny took her hand. "*Liebling*, he won't hurt you. You can trust him."

The group approached an elevator, where Harry pushed the

button labeled "P." The doors slid open, revealing the portal to the outside world. It showed them a camp hidden in the forest. Everafters were chopping down trees, building houses, and carving spears.

"Look, there's Billy now," Daphne said.

The former mayor and his diminutive assistant, Mr. Seven, were poring over maps and plans. Seven was one of the world-famous seven dwarfs, and despite his boss's frequent insults, he was always at Charming's side. Sabrina wondered what kept him so loyal now that the prince could no longer afford to pay his salary.

"This is foolish," Henry warned. "Charming can't be trusted."

"Harry, it was a pleasure to meet you. You've been a real help," Granny said, shaking his hand. She then sent Poppa Bear through the portal with Uncle Jake on his back.

Harry grinned and waved good-bye as the rest of the group followed the bear through the portal. "Come back soon. We've always got a room for you."

The world on the other side of the portal couldn't have been more different from the Hotel of Wonders. Sabrina found herself inside a crude log cabin with a dirt floor and a thatched roof. A few stools were scattered around a rough table with a scale model of Ferryport Landing resting at its center. Charming and Seven were startled by the group's sudden arrival.

"Whoa! Incoming!" a face cried as it appeared inside another mirror leaning against the opposite wall. This guardian had dark brown skin and long, untamed dreadlocks. He wore big round sunglasses with peace signs in the lenses.

"You can relax, Reggie," Charming said. "They're friends."

"T'is a good t'ing, but can I get a warning next time? You gon' give a man a heart attack," Reggie said, and then vanished.

"Relda, are there more coming through?" Charming asked. "Or is it safe to say you've already brought the entire town?"

"It's nice to see you, too, William," she replied. "We'll be out of your hair as quickly as we came. Jacob is injured, shot by one of Nottingham's arrows. He needs medical attention immediately," Granny Relda pleaded.

"Seven, can you take the bear with Jacob to the medical tent?" Charming asked.

Mr. Seven hurried Poppa Bear out of the cabin to get Jake the help he needed.

"Don't worry. Nurse Sprat will take care of your boy, Relda," Charming said.

"Thank you, William. Jake was attacked by the Hand when they came to our house demanding information about this . . . this . . . Well, what, exactly, are you building here?"

Charming led the group out into an open courtyard. Sabrina was stunned by what she saw. The image she'd seen in the mirror didn't do the place justice. Charming's "camp" was actually a huge fort with outer walls over twenty-five feet high. The compound was large enough to fit dozens of cabins, a mess tent, a makeshift hospital, an armory, and a small farm. Hundreds of Everafters were busy gardening, working with horses, and building more barracks.

"Welcome to Camp Charming," the prince announced proudly. "The Everafters' last stand against the Scarlet Hand."

3

L OOK FAMILIAR?" DAPHNE ASKED SABRINA.

An icy feeling crept along her back. Sabrina couldn't believe her eyes. The fortress was nearly identical to the one the sisters had visited during their trip to the future. Like this one, it was built to fight the Scarlet Hand. The girls and Charming had worked hard to make sure that particular future didn't happen. But, clearly, they hadn't changed it enough. Perhaps there was no way to avoid their dark destiny: war.

"The Scarlet Hand is harassing Everafters, especially ones who associate with your family. I built this camp as a safe haven, and we've had a steady flow of people seeking shelter," Charming explained.

"How did you build this so fast?" Granny Relda asked. "You and Mr. Canis fled into the forest only yesterday!"

"We work fast around here," a voice said from behind them.

They spun around to find Mr. Canis approaching. He was as unkempt as ever and now sported a black patch over his left eye. He gestured toward a wizard levitating a load of rubble with a magic wand. He was helping construct a well.

Daphne wrapped Mr. Canis up in a hug. He almost toppled over but steadied himself with the cane he now carried.

The cane bothered Sabrina. Canis had never needed one before. He looked weak and frail, but he seemed at peace with himself. An easy smile had replaced his trademark scowl. "It's good to see you, child," he said to Daphne, then turned his attention to Sabrina's parents. "Henry and Veronica, welcome. I am pleased to see you up and about."

"Goldilocks woke them up," Daphne said. "With a smooch!"

Puck stuck out his tongue and gagged loudly.

Granny took Canis by the hand. "How are you feeling, old friend?"

"A little tired." He shook his cane. "It appears I am not a young man anymore."

There was a long, uncomfortable pause.

"Canis, did you just tell a joke?" Henry asked.

Canis shrugged. "I tried."

"Wow," Veronica said. "We've missed a lot, haven't we?"

"Yoga and meditation have been invaluable to me. Now that I'm free, I'm starting to remember my life before I became the

Wolf, slowly but surely," he said, stepping close to Red Riding Hood. He held his hand out to her in friendship. "I believe it might work for you, too. If you're willing."

Red didn't take his hand. She hid behind Granny Relda's leg, trembling. It was clear that she was still terrified of the old man. The monster that used to control him had killed her grandmother. She, herself, had been under the power of a similar creature until the Grimms cured them both, setting the story straight. But, all of this had happened very recently. Sabrina couldn't blame Red if she wasn't immediately ready to hang out with the guy who ate her grandma.

"Perhaps another time," the old man said, and then he turned back to Granny Relda. "I'm told that Jacob has been attacked."

Granny nodded. "The Hand surrounded the house, and Nottingham shot him with an arrow when he confronted them."

Canis turned to Charming. "You predicted that tensions would escalate."

"I'm rarely wrong," Charming said, matter-of-factly. "This violence is further evidence that turning the refugees into an army is our best chance of survival."

"An army?" Goldilocks cried.

"It's clear that the tide is turning toward war. The Hand has taken over the town and run all the humans out. They're hunting down anyone who doesn't agree with them. We need to prepare."

"And once you beat the Hand, you can point your little army toward taking over the town for yourself?" Henry challenged.

Charming sneered. "I liked you better when you were asleep."

"What does Snow think of this?" Granny Relda said, referring to the prince's on-again, off-again girlfriend. Sabrina wondered the same thing. She couldn't imagine Ms. White supporting a war effort. She taught a fierce self-defense class called the Bad Apples, but Ms. White spent most of class time teaching her students how to block attackers and avoid a fight.

"Ask her yourself," the prince said, gesturing to an open stretch of field near the far wall of the camp. There, Sabrina saw two dozen Everafters doing pushups in the mud. Snow White stood over them, shouting commands and blasting a whistle.

"I can't believe it!" Goldilocks cried.

"Ms. White is in charge of the camp's security, and she's drafted a few of our guests to help out. Unfortunately, our community is a collection of feeble morons. Ms. White has her work cut out for her."

"Ms. White?" Daphne said.

"Trouble in paradise, Billy?" Sabrina asked.

The prince lowered his eyes. "She and I are not on speaking terms," he mumbled. "If you'll excuse me, Mr. Seven and I have to dig up some extra cots. The refugees keep coming, and supplies are growing scarce."

They marched across the field, leaving the group behind.

"I suppose you would like to say hello to our resident drill sergeant?" Canis said, gesturing toward Snow White and her rag-tag crew of soon-to-be soldiers. He led them toward the group. As they got closer, Sabrina noticed that the former teacher was dressed in full army fatigues. Her recruits ran in place. She called them "worthless," "weak," and "spineless maggots."

"Snow! What in heaven?" Granny cried.

"Getting these plebes into shape," Ms. White said, never taking her eyes off her troops. "Have you come to volunteer? We can use all the soldiers we can get."

"Oh, no! I think I'm a little too old to go to war," Granny replied.

"That's a shame. How about you, Henry?" Snow said. "Now that you're up and at 'em, you could make yourself useful. It would be nice to have one of the Grimm boys helping out."

Henry shook his head vigorously. "We're leaving town as soon as we can."

"Can't say I blame you," Snow replied. "No one is safe here. Homes are being searched without warrants, property is being re-possessed without cause, not to mention the disappearances . . . Relda, your son has a point. I'd go with him, if I were you."

"I'm not leaving," Granny Relda said firmly.

Henry scowled.

"So, what's the scoop on you and the prince?" Daphne asked.

"Daphne! Don't be rude," Veronica admonished.

"No worries, Veronica. The girls have been privy to my soap opera of a romantic life for quite some time. If you must know, Billy proposed."

"Gravy!" Daphne cried.

"And I declined," Snow added.

"What? Why?" Granny asked.

"Well, he's arrogant. He's mean. He's selfish," Sabrina said.

"Sabrina, that's not nice," Veronica said.

"She's not wrong," Henry said.

A gray goose hobbled over to the group. "A new group of refugees has just arrived, Snow, and one of them is asking for Geppetto," it honked.

"Geppetto, front and center!" Snow demanded as she turned back to her troops. An elderly man covered in mud fell out of formation and ran to Snow White. He saluted her nervously.

"Yes, sir!" he shouted.

"Geppetto!" Granny cried. "You're training to be a soldier?"

Geppetto nodded. "Absolutely. I want to do my part. My toy store is ashes, anyway. They burned it to the ground when I refused to take an oath to the Hand. It's time to fight back."

The rest of the troops let out an exuberant "Hoo-ah!"

"Well, it appears you have a visitor, maggot," Snow shouted, though there wasn't enough venom in her voice to really make the insult believable. "Let's go see who it is."

Everyone followed Snow and Geppetto across camp. A throng of excited Everafters gathered in the courtyard to welcome the new refugees. When they entered the gate, they were met with hugs and cheers. Sabrina and Daphne squirmed their way to the front and watched the reunions. Geppetto reported to King Arthur, who held a list of people entering the fort.

"Sir, I was told there is someone looking for me?"

"Oh, yes, the kid. Over there." He pointed.

Sabrina spotted a small boy sitting on an overstuffed traveling bag. He appeared no older than Daphne and wore a pair of red overalls and a button-down shirt. A quail feather stuck out from his yellow hat. His face was angular, his nose a bit pointy, and he had a pronounced overbite. His expression was tired and impatient until his gaze landed on Geppetto. At once, his face split into a wide, toothy grin.

"Papa!" he cried. "Dearest Papa!"

"Papa?" Sabrina and Daphne repeated.

"Son? Is it you?" Tears gushed from the corners of Geppetto's eyes. He rushed to the child and, in one quick motion, scooped him off the ground and swung him around in his arms. "You've come back," Geppetto sobbed.

"Is that . . . Is that . . . ?" Daphne couldn't finish her question. She was biting down hard on the palm of her hand.

"Pinocchio!" Henry exclaimed. "That's *the* Pinocchio?"

"Yes, *liebling*. It appears Pinocchio has finally returned," Granny Relda said, a happy tear sliding down her cheek. Geppetto was a family friend, and the Grimms knew the toy-maker's heart had been broken the day he was separated from his son, nearly two hundred years ago.

"Gravy," Red said.

Sabrina wanted to be happy for Geppetto, but an odd bitterness stabbed at her heart. Instead of joy, she felt envy. His family reunion was filled with delight, while her own was less than perfect. She looked to her father, hoping the scene wouldn't be lost on him. But, he was busy talking to King Arthur about possible ways out of the forest.

"My little pine seed, where have you been?" Geppetto asked his son. "Why didn't you get on the boat with me? I've been a mess for so long, worrying about you."

"I'll explain it all in good time, Papa," Pinocchio said. "Just let me embrace you one more time!"

"He talks funny," Puck said. The boy had a thick Italian accent, and his words had an air of sophistication, like he was an adult rather than a little kid.

"You smell funny," Sabrina grumbled.

Puck raised an arm and sniffed his armpit. "Can't argue with you there."

"I thought Pinocchio was a puppet," Daphne said to her grandmother.

"He was," Granny Relda said. "But after he proved he could be good, the Blue Fairy granted his greatest wish—to be a real boy."

"Where has he been all this time?" Goldilocks wondered.

"Arthur has given me directions to a path that will take us out of the woods," Henry interrupted. "Girls, say your good-byes. We're leaving."

"But Uncle Jake is hurt!" Daphne said. "Besides, that's Pinocchio. I want to get his autograph."

"Daphne, I've had enough of your back talk," Henry snapped. "Be a big girl and get your suitcases. We left them in Charming's hut."

Daphne huffed and stomped off toward the cabin.

"Relda, are you sure you won't come with us?" Veronica begged.

"Veronica, you know I can't go," Granny said. "If the family abandons Ferryport Landing, the barrier will fall, and this chaos will spill out into the surrounding towns. The Everafters need us now more than ever."

"Jacob is still here," Henry said. "When he feels better, he can take over the responsibility."

"Jacob is a free spirit. I'm surprised he's stayed as long as he has," Granny said. "No, the responsibility is mine."

"At least go back to the house," Henry begged. "The protection spells will prevent anyone from getting inside. A hurricane could hit that house, and you'd still be safe. Just don't get involved with this. Wait until it all blows over. I don't want you to end up like Dad."

Granny Relda's face fell with disappointment, but Henry either didn't notice or chose to ignore it.

"I'll let you know where we end up," he continued, then turned to call to Daphne, who was dragging the suitcases with great effort. "C'mon, Daphne, don't dillydally! We've got a train to catch!"

Daphne slammed Sabrina's suitcase to the ground. "Carry your own bag, traitor."

"What did I do?" Sabrina cried.

Daphne ignored her. She hugged Granny and Mr. Canis and said good-bye to the others. Then, she stomped off to wait by the gate.

"So, I guess I'll see you when I see you," Puck said to Sabrina.

"Yeah, I guess," she muttered. As much as she wanted to leave Ferryport Landing, it didn't feel right to go now. Not with a war brewing. Some of the Everafters might be hurt. Granny might need them. Puck might need them.

"C'mon, Sabrina," her father said, grabbing her suitcase and leading her and Veronica to the main gates. Seconds later, they were marching out into the forest, leaving the camp behind.

Sabrina looked back one more time just as the gates closed.

Puck stood in the entrance, hands on hips, his wings flapping in the sun. Granny was next to him, smiling through tears. Red stood next to her, trembling in fear. Goldilocks handed Granny a handkerchief, and Momma Bear wrapped a furry arm around her shoulders. Mr. Canis leaned on his cane.

I should thank them, Sabrina thought. *I should tell them that I love them.* But the gates closed before she could utter a single word.

They traipsed through the woods, seemingly without any sense of direction. Sabrina thought she'd seen most of the forest surrounding Ferryport Landing—after all, she had been chased through it by enough monsters—but nothing looked familiar. She hoped they weren't lost. It wasn't long before Henry was forced to stop and consult the crude map he had gotten from King Arthur. When Veronica offered help, he held up his hand for silence.

"He's like this in the car, too," Veronica muttered as she watched her husband turn the map over and over.

Daphne sat on a stump and sulked, her head tilted downward.

"Well, that's new," Veronica said to Sabrina. "I don't think I've ever seen your sister angry."

"Stick around," Sabrina replied. "It's pretty regular these days."

"You two have changed so much." Veronica sighed.

"We've been through a lot," Sabrina said. "We had to adapt."

Henry tucked his map into his pocket. "OK, I know where

we are. It'll take about two hours to get to the train station, if we hurry." He checked his watch. "We should be able to catch the 6:17 to Grand Central."

"So, Henry, we're just going to stumble into New York City with no money and no place to sleep? That's your plan?" Veronica asked.

Henry shook his head. "I have some money—enough to get us a hotel for the night. Tomorrow we can tackle our bank accounts."

"Tomorrow is Sunday," Veronica said. "The banks will be closed."

Henry stumbled but righted himself quickly. "I'll figure something out."

"Daphne and I slept in plenty of homeless shelters when we ran away from foster families," Sabrina offered. "I know which places will take us."

"Oh, goody!" Veronica cried, sarcastically. "Our problems have been solved!"

Henry fumed. "I would rather have us sleeping in a gutter before we spend another night in this forsaken town! I know you don't agree with how I'm doing it, but I'm going to protect this family. I can't do that if we're in Ferryport Landing, surrounded by this Everafter craziness. And to be perfectly clear, I don't want anyone in this family around any Everafters. And that includes the ones who live in New York City!"

Veronica's face fell. "You were eavesdropping?"

"You lied to me!"

"I had to! I knew you wouldn't approve, and I was trying to help. Isn't that what Grimms do?"

"Don't throw that silly catchphrase at me," Henry snapped.

"Well." Veronica steeled herself. "Now that the secret's out, you must know that there are at least two hundred Everafters running around Manhattan. So, if you're trying to get away from them—"

"Not a problem," Henry interrupted. "We're moving."

"Moving!" Sabrina gasped, appalled. Moving away from New York City was not part of the dream reunion she had been imagining.

"Yes, we'll move far away! To somewhere no Everafter would want to live!"

"Like where?"

"I don't know. Canton, maybe."

"Canton, Ohio!" Veronica groaned. "No one wants to live in Canton, Ohio! *I* don't want to live in Canton, Ohio!"

"It doesn't matter where we move, as long as it's boring," Henry shouted. "We'll find someplace where the mayor isn't royalty and the local police aren't magical transforming pigs!"

"Actually, the Sheriff of Nottingham is running the police department now," Sabrina corrected.

"I miss Elvis," Daphne whimpered.

Veronica turned to face her husband. "So, you're laying down the law, huh? Do I get a say in any of this, or am I supposed to play the dutiful wife? Perhaps you'd like me to put on an apron and make you a pot roast, too?"

Henry scowled. "Veronica, that's a bit dramatic."

"I miss Elvis," Daphne repeated.

"You're not going to drag me and the girls through this world, hiding from pixies and fairy godmothers. They're out there, and most of them are not bad people."

"Pixies are not people," Henry snapped. "And don't you try to tell me about Everafters. I've lived side by side with them most of my life. My mother's best friend is one! I used to be in love with one!"

"I'm painfully aware of your love life, Henry Grimm." Veronica seethed. "I woke up this morning from a two-year sleep to find your old girlfriend sitting over you with her big moon eyes!"

"Veronica! I can't believe you're jealous," Henry whined.

Sabrina didn't know much about adult relationships, but she was pretty sure it was a mistake to accuse your wife of being jealous of an old girlfriend. Her mother looked like a volcano preparing to explode.

"JEALOUS?!"

Henry sputtered. "I didn't exactly mean—"

"What do I have to be jealous about?" she cried. "I'm the best thing that ever happened to you, pal! You hit the lottery when you met me! I'm smart. I'm funny. I can throw a sixty-mile-an-hour fastball! And, I'm a babe!"

Henry's face turned bright red. "I am the luckiest man in the world."

"You've got that right!" she cried, and after a moment she took a deep breath and continued. "Henry, we're still a family—a team—and we're supposed to make decisions together. There has to be a smarter way to keep all of us safe. I—wait, where's Daphne?"

Sabrina spun around, but her sister was nowhere to be found. "She must have gone back to see Elvis."

"Wait here. I'll go get her," Henry said. He took off running back the way they'd come, leaving Veronica and Sabrina alone. They shared a glance and then raced after him. Henry's voice rang through the forest. He called out for Daphne, demanding she come back, but he was wasting his breath. Daphne was stubborn—maybe even more stubborn than Sabrina—and when she wanted to do something, there was no talking her out of it.

When Sabrina and Veronica finally caught up with Henry, he was standing with Daphne in a clearing of trees with his hand clamped around her arm.

"This is unacceptable, young lady," he scolded.

"I'm not leaving," Daphne said. "They need us."

"What makes you think you can do anything to help?" Henry demanded. "You're only five years old!"

"Dad, she's seven," Sabrina corrected.

"Eight in two weeks!" Daphne snapped. "And, I've fought plenty of bad guys in the last year. I'm a Grimm. This is what I do!"

Just then, no fewer than a dozen hulking figures stepped out from behind the trees, surrounding the family. They each stood nearly seven feet tall, with bumpy gray skin like that of an alligator. Their eyes were enormous and bloodshot, and their ears were pointy and covered in what looked like porcupine quills. A few held long spears, and others clung to clubs with dozens of rusty spikes nailed into them. Sabrina recognized them as hobgoblins.

One of the monsters stepped forward. His chest was decorated in gaudy medals and his face in scars. Like all of the hobgoblins, his chest was painted with the mark of the Scarlet Hand. He surveyed the Grimms, and then his face lit up with a sick grin.

"I knew I recognized the foul stink that comes off humans, but I never suspected we'd find ones who are so famous," he said.

"You want an autograph?" Sabrina grumbled. Henry shot her a look that told her to keep her mouth shut.

A second monster lumbered forward to join his leader. "They must be coming from Charming's camp," he said. "They've allied themselves with the traitor and his troublemakers."

"That means it must be nearby," the leader crowed. He turned back to the family and gnashed his crooked, yellow teeth. "Now, let's avoid any unpleasantness, shall we? Tell us where the camp is."

"We don't have any idea what you're talking about," Henry lied. "We're not coming from any camp. My family and I are just out for a picnic."

The hobgoblin leaped forward until his face was only an inch from Henry's. "You're lying. All of you Grimms lie."

"That's not a very nice thing to say," Henry said. "I'm hurt."

"If you don't tell me where the camp is, there's a lot more hurt coming."

Henry shook his head. "We've gotten off on the wrong foot. Let's start over. My family is not involved with Charming. We have refused to take a side in your conflict, and we are on our way to the train station now. So, if you'll kindly step aside and let us pass, we'll get out of your hair."

"You'll go where I tell you, human," the monster snorted, and then turned to his men. "Bind their hands. If they won't tell us where the fort is, we'll beat the answer out of them, starting with the children."

One of the hobgoblins clamped his hands down on Sabrina's arms. She tried to pull free, but he was too strong. She stomped her heel down hard on his exposed toes, and he yelped in agony.

"Why, you little terror. I'm going to tear your arms off and hit you with them," he threatened.

There was a flash of fists and feet, loud groans, and the cracking of bones. At first, Sabrina couldn't tell who had arrived to rescue them, but it soon became clear that her mother and father had leaped into action.

Henry was like a tornado, whipping from one hobgoblin to the next, planting punches with incredible accuracy. The way he fought looked like dancing; he was kicking and punching to a rhythm only he could hear.

Veronica was not quite so elegant. She snatched a thick branch off the forest floor and clubbed anyone who got close. Sabrina remembered one evening when her parents took her to the boardwalk at Coney Island. At the batting cages, Henry and Veronica decided to see who could hit the most fastballs. Veronica won by a landslide, smacking the balls hard into the netting. The monsters' ribs and heads weren't nearly as hard as baseballs, but she swung for the fences anyway. Working together, Henry and Veronica managed to take out eight of the monsters.

Sabrina looked over at her sister. "Our parents are so gravy."

Daphne scowled. "That's not how you say it."

"Girls, run for the camp!" Henry shouted as he fought off a hobgoblin who was charging at him with a spear in hand.

"No, we can help," Daphne challenged, assuming the fighting stance she'd learned in Ms. White's self-defense class.

"Listen to your father!" Veronica cried, smashing her branch into the belly of one of the beasts and knocking him to the ground.

Sabrina snatched her sister by the hand and pulled her down the path toward the fortress.

"We have to go back!" Daphne said. "We can't just leave them."

"Our parents are tough," Sabrina said, doing her best to sound confident. "They'll be right behind us."

The girls ran and ran. By the time they came to Charming's camp, Sabrina was so spent, she could barely shout for help. A sentry appeared in a tower and aimed a magic wand at them. "Stand back, invaders!" he shouted, as blast of white-hot fire exploded at Sabrina's feet.

"Open the gate!" Sabrina cried. "It's Sabrina and Daphne Grimm! Monsters are chasing us!"

The sentry blew a whistle, and the big gates swung open.

Before the girls could take a single step inside, a regiment of knights on horseback charged past them. The girls were nearly trampled before Charming rushed to their side with his silver sword in hand. He snatched Sabrina by the arm. "Where are these monsters?" he shouted.

Sabrina pointed back the way they'd come. "There are at least a dozen, maybe more. They're attacking my mom and dad."

"You fools! You may have led them to us," he cried in disgust.

"Freaky monsters were trying to kill us," Sabrina said. "Should we have just died out there so you could keep your clubhouse secret?"

"Absolutely!" the prince said.

"I knew you'd come back," Puck said, as she strolled through the gate. "You got it bad for me, don't you?"

Sabrina would have slugged the fairy boy, but just then Henry and Veronica appeared, looking slightly worse for wear. Henry's lip was bloody, and Veronica had a long scratch on her right arm.

"How many were there?" Charming demanded.

"Fourteen that we saw," Henry replied. "They're hobgoblins. We managed to subdue twelve of them. If you walk along the path, you'll find them."

"And the other two?"

"They ran," Veronica said, still clinging to her heavy branch. "Cowards."

Charming pulled a knight aside and ordered him to gather as many of the Merry Men as he could. "Find those hobgoblins. If they get back to the Hand, they'll reveal where we are, and we'll be overrun by nightfall!"

A moment later, a well-armed posse of archers and swordsmen was racing out into the forest.

4

BEFORE NIGHTFALL, THE CAMP RECEIVED MORE than three dozen new Everafter refugees. They looked tired and broken. Many shared tales of brutal beatings, threats, and murder.

Mr. Canis called them "guests" and informed them that in joining the camp they had an obligation to all the other refugees. Each person would be assigned tasks the next morning based on their occupations or talents, but until then they should try to get some rest and something to eat. Robin Hood's wife, Marian, led the newcomers on a tour and then to the supply tent for fresh clothes. She promised hot meals and clean bunks.

Charming marched through the camp spreading news of the hobgoblin attack. The story seemed to startle everyone, especially the recent arrivals.

"The Hand is bringing the fight to us!" the prince said. "It's time to prepare for war."

But his call to action didn't produce his desired response. He was largely ignored. Many of the Everafters said they didn't want to get involved, even if they were shaken by the prince's dark predictions. By the end of the day, only six more refugees had volunteered to join Snow White's militia.

Dinner was served in the courtyard as the sun sank below the tree line. Morgan le Fey conjured enough tables and folding chairs for everyone. The magic tables came complete with plates, utensils, and drinking glasses. Mr. Seven lit torches so everyone could see. The refugees stood in a long line for their share of beans, brown bread, potatoes, and corn.

Sabrina and her family, along with Red, dined together. Granny Relda invited Mr. Canis to join, but he claimed he needed to get back to his meditation. Goldilocks and her bears were invited as well, but Goldie seemed nervous around Henry, and she said that they were going to help in the kitchen. Geppetto and Pinocchio, however, happily accepted the invite.

"Good evening, all," Pinocchio said. "My father has spoken highly of your family. He considers you some of his dearest friends. I'm quite honored to make your acquaintance."

Sabrina couldn't help staring at Pinocchio. If the story was true, Geppetto had carved him from a solid block of wood, but now he was flesh and blood. What threw her the most about the boy wasn't his magical transformation, but how he spoke to everyone. He was so proper and mature, but he looked so young.

"Nice to meet you, too," Granny Relda said. "Your father has told us endless stories about you. He's a very proud papa."

"Indeed," Geppetto said, giving the boy a hug.

"So, where have you been?" Puck asked the odd little boy.

"That's a little rude," Veronica said.

Puck let out a tremendous belch. "You think so?"

"It's not much of a tale, I'm afraid," the little boy said.

"Then skip it," Puck said, piling beans into his mouth. "We've spent entirely too much time discussing things other than me."

Granny rolled her eyes. "Puck, please. Let Pinocchio speak."

"Very well. I'm confident Papa told you about our missed connection aboard the Grimm vessel."

"What's a vessel?" Daphne asked.

"The layman calls it a boat," Pinocchio explained.

"What's a layman?" Daphne asked.

"Oh dear. The schools in this town are failing the youth," Pinocchio said.

Daphne frowned but said nothing.

"I have never cared for the sea after a very disturbing encounter with a great white shark. I also had a bit of trouble on an island off the coast of Italy where children were transformed into donkeys. Thus, I prefer to stay landlocked whenever possible."

"I wonder how hard it would be to hide a shark under someone's pillow," Puck whispered to Sabrina. She shook a threatening fist at him.

"So I returned to Italy and took a few odd jobs," Pinocchio continued. "I was an apprentice at a newspaper and learned to work a printing press. The paper wasn't much to speak of—mostly propaganda—but it was a valuable trade until I was forced to move on."

"Oh dear, what happened?" his father asked.

"It's this infernal spell the Blue Fairy put on me. It made me a real boy, but it prevents me from growing any older. To avoid anyone noticing, I had to move on frequently, unable to put down any roots or get ahead in a profession. I made the horrible blunder of sticking around for too long once in Eastern Europe, and the superstitious townspeople chased me with torches and pitchforks. Do yourself a favor and stay away from Transylvania."

"Oh, but that's not because of the spell. It's 'cause you're an Everafter. You have to decide to get older, or you'll stay the same age forever," Daphne explained.

"Alas, no," the boy replied. "My condition is unique even amongst my people. I believe I am trapped at this age due to the wish the Blue Fairy granted. I asked to be a real boy. Not to be a real boy who grows into a man."

"You have to be real specific with wishes," Sabrina said, sympathetically.

"The Blue Fairy lives here in town," Daphne said. "We could help you find her. Maybe she could fix the wish."

"Thank you, but no," Pinocchio said. "Like your sister said, her wish granting leaves a little to be desired. If I asked her to let me grow up, she'd probably make it so that I grew all the way to the moon. I'll seek other options."

"It wasn't all bad now, pine seed," Geppetto said, continuing the story. "He's had quite a life and has gotten to see beautiful parts of the world. He was an artist's assistant in Spain and sold kites in the markets in Paris. He lived in the Taj Mahal for a month before security guards found him. And, he was a shoeshine boy on the Orient Express."

"It sounds like an adventure," Henry said.

"I guess it could be seen in that manner," Pinocchio said. "Papa, I believe I found the magical forest of enchanted wood you used to carve my original body."

"Marvelous!" Geppetto said, clapping his hands. "I thought those woods were destroyed by a forest fire."

"Unfortunately, what you heard is true. Shortly after I discovered it, every tree was consumed by a mysterious blaze."

"How tragic," his father said.

"I'd like to know how you ended up here in the camp," Henry pressed.

Pinocchio shifted uncomfortably. "I had a great deal of savings from my many occupations, so I purchased an airplane ticket on the Internet. I landed in New York City and boarded the next train for Ferryport Landing. Once I arrived, it was clear that trouble was afoot, but I searched for my father nonetheless. During my inquiries, I met a young man who led me here. He was quite peculiar. He has a pumpkin for a head."

"Jack Pumpkinhead," Granny said. "He's from Oz. They're all a little peculiar."

"I couldn't be happier, pine seed." Geppetto beamed. "After dinner you must show everyone your marionettes."

Granny smiled. "So you are a puppet-maker as well?"

"Like father, like son," Geppetto said, beaming with pride.

They hugged again. Sabrina looked over at her own father, who was busy studying his map of the town. It was clear he was looking for another way out of Ferryport Landing.

Nurse Sprat approached the table. She wore a smock with a red cross on the front. She had once worked at the Ferryport Landing Memorial Hospital, where she had been responsible for looking after Red Riding Hood during the height of her mental illness. When she spotted Red among the group, she paused for a moment, then approached.

"Jacob is going to be fine," she announced.

"Thank goodness," Granny cried.

"Normally, a wound like his would take a couple of months to heal, but, well, I left him alone for a minute, and when I returned, he was smearing a black salve all over his shoulder. Whatever it is, it performs miracles. He should be shipshape in a couple of days.

Relda, if your family has any more of that medicine, it would come in very handy around here."

Granny smiled. "I'll do my best to find you some."

"Can we see him?" Henry asked.

"Tomorrow," Nurse Sprat said. "He's sleeping now."

"Thank you so much, Mrs. Sprat," Granny said.

"You're welcome." She glanced at Red but said nothing, and then she returned to her medical tent.

"Well, it appears we have even more to celebrate," Geppetto crowed.

A loud bell rang, and the gates of the fort opened. Robin Hood and his men marched inside, leading the hobgoblins Henry and Veronica had pummeled earlier that day. The brutes were bound at the wrists with heavy chains. They grunted and complained as they were roughly shoved along. Charming appeared and ordered the men to lock all of the creatures in his cabin, and he asked Little John to make sure they were guarded twenty-four hours a day. "We can't have them escape. Especially not before we question them."

"You won't get anything out of us," the hobgoblin leader said.

Snow White stepped into the courtyard, still in her military fatigues. She cracked her knuckles loudly. "We'll just see about that."

"Relda, you seem to have a knack for gathering useful information. Could you help Snow?" Charming asked.

"My mother is not part of your war," Henry said.

Granny stood up. "Henry, don't be rude. Of course I'll do what I can."

Sabrina watched her father seethe.

After dinner, the group dispersed. Sabrina and Daphne decided to give their parents some privacy. It was clear another argument was brewing.

Puck accompanied them as they wandered aimlessly around the fort, taking in all the different Everafters and the work being done. They stopped when Daphne spotted Red Riding Hood hiding behind Charming's cabin. She rushed over and sat down next to her.

"Hey," Daphne said.

"Hey." Red forced a smile onto her face.

"Are you hiding back here?"

"I'm trying to stay out of the way. I don't want to be any trouble."

"I'm all about trouble," Puck offered.

"You're not trouble, Red," Daphne said. "Granny invited you to live with us, so that makes you part of our family. You don't have to run off and hide."

She turned to Sabrina, clearly hoping she would agree. Instead, Sabrina studied a dusty rock by her foot. She wasn't ready to accept the little girl, not after everything that had happened. She wasn't even ready to pretend.

"Mrs. Grimm is very kind," Red said.

"She's gravy," Daphne agreed. "Plus she's an excellent cook—"

Sabrina laughed out loud, and Daphne flashed her an angry look.

"Well, you shouldn't lie to her," Sabrina said defensively.

Daphne turned back to Red. "Like I was saying . . . you're one of us. Soon, you will have your own room. Granny promised to build me one, too. Maybe you and I could have a secret door that leads between them—one only we know about."

"I would like that," Red said, grinning.

Sabrina was stung. Daphne had refused to share a bedroom with her, but she was hoping her sister would get over her anger. Sabrina knew it had been wrong to lie to Daphne about the horn of the North Wind, but they were sisters! Wasn't blood thicker than water? Wasn't Daphne supposed to forgive her?

Prince Charming's voice boomed from a window directly above them. Sabrina couldn't quite make out what he was shouting.

"What's going on?" Red asked.

"Let's find out," Sabrina said as she stretched to her tiptoes to peek into the window. The rest of the children followed suit, elbowing each other for the best view.

Inside, they saw a hobgoblin sitting on a chair. His hands were bound behind him. His face was both tired and angry. Charming and Snow hovered over him. Granny sat in a chair across from him, her hands resting patiently in her lap. Mr. Canis and Mr. Seven looked on.

"What does the Master know about this camp?" Charming demanded.

The hobgoblin spat at him, "Nothing yet, traitor. But you're a fool if you think you can hide anything from him for long."

"You speak of the Master as if you know him. Who is he?" Granny Relda asked.

Sabrina's heart skipped a beat. She, too, had wondered about the Master's identity. She often feared she had walked past him on the street, or—worse—that he was someone she knew.

The hobgoblin snorted a laugh. "I haven't earned the honor of meeting him, but one day I will prove my worth and kneel at his feet."

"So you take orders from someone you have never even met?" Snow asked.

"His is a glorious plan for Everafters," he barked at her. "That is all I need to know."

"Not all Everafters," Ms. White corrected him. "Only the ones willing to lick his boots."

"It's you that turned your back on Everafters when you allied yourself with the Grimms and the rest of the human filth," the hobgoblin said. "These are the very people responsible for our imprisonment. You should not befriend them, Snow White. You should help us exterminate them."

"So that's the Master's plan?" Charming pressed. "Murder the Grimms?"

"No, he has found another solution to break us out of this tired, little town," the commander said smugly. "He will destroy the barrier that traps us, and we will march freely across the nations, recapturing the lands and treasures that are rightfully ours."

"And I suppose enslaving the world is part of the plan, too?" Mr. Canis asked.

"Naturally," the hobgoblin said.

Charming rolled his eyes. "I've heard enough from this fool. Was he searched?"

Mr. Seven stepped forward and handed Charming a filthy burlap sack. The prince emptied it onto a nearby table, and the group gathered around to study each item: a rusty dagger covered in dried blood, a couple of loaves of moldy bread, a compass, a map of the woods, and a small pocket mirror. Charming held up the mirror with a smirk. "I had no idea hobgoblins were so vain."

The hobgoblin chuckled. There was something arrogant in his laugh, as if he knew a secret.

Charming turned to Granny Relda. "Mrs. Grimm, I have a favor to ask."

The children stepped back from the window.

"What were they talking about?" Daphne asked. "I couldn't see or hear anything."

"The Master," Red said.

"Ugh, gross," Daphne said.

"He wants to take over the world," Puck added. "Been there. Done that."

"Did they say who the Master is?" Daphne asked.

Puck shook his head. "Not even a clue."

"Wait a minute," Sabrina said, turning to Red. "Haven't you seen the Master?"

Red Riding Hood looked to the ground and shuffled her feet.

"You told us that you talked to him when you attacked us with the Jabberwocky," Sabrina pressed.

"I don't remember," the child said in a small voice.

"Sure, you do," Sabrina said. She was so excited, she could hardly talk. "Just think. If you tell us who he is, then Charming can send people to capture him. And no one else will be hurt!"

"It's blurry." The little girl clutched her head in her hands, as if straining to remember were causing her physical pain. "I don't think I can."

Sabrina grabbed her by the shoulders. "You have to!"

Daphne stepped between them. "Sabrina, chill out! She says she doesn't remember."

"She's not trying," Sabrina said.

"She is trying, but your bullying isn't helping," Puck added. "Her memory is messed up. Don't you remember what Canis said? He can't remember big parts of his life when the wolf was inside of him. It's the same with Red. We'll have to think of some other way to figure out who the Master is."

Sabrina was furious. Who was he to call her a bully?

"Maybe you should let me do the thinking around here, Puck," she snapped. "I'd hate to burn out that little peanut in your head."

"You wish you were as smart as me. I'm brilliant," Puck said, puffing up his chest.

Sabrina's face twisted in anger. "Brilliantly stinky. I doubt too many people would list themselves as exceptional when their greatest talent is eating with their feet!"

Red watched, bewildered. "Are you two in love or something?"

Daphne started to laugh but clamped her hand over her mouth when both Sabrina and Puck glared at her. Maybe it was Daphne's amusement, or Red's embarrassing question, but— before she could stop herself—Sabrina blurted out the one thing she swore she'd never admit.

"In love? As if! How on earth he and I end up married is beyond me! I don't know how my future self held her nose long enough to get through the ceremony. Ugh!"

Everyone fell silent. Daphne stood in shock. Red looked bewildered.

"MARRIED?" Puck cried, his eyes as big as his head.

Sabrina was sure she was going to hyperventilate. She closed her eyes and prayed for another rip in time—one that would allow her to go back ten seconds and kick herself in the rear before she opened her mouth. But no black hole appeared to whisk her away.

"Tell me," Puck said.

"It's nothing," Sabrina mumbled.

"TELL ME!"

"I was kidding," she lied, but she barely got it out before Puck's wings appeared. He snatched her in his arms, and soon they were both flying up into the air.

"Tell me what you know about the future!" he shouted.

"Fine! Do you remember when Cinderella's husband built the time machine that nearly ate the town? Well, Daphne and I got pulled into it and saw the future and—"

"NO!" Puck cried, suddenly understanding what she was telling him.

"We were married in the future!" Sabrina confirmed. "Listen, I'm no happier about it than you."

"You're lying! I'm a little boy. Little boys do not get married."

"You grew up."

Puck's face fell. "What would make me do that?"

Sabrina cringed. "Me."

"I would never do that!" Puck roared.

"You're already doing it," Sabrina said. "Haven't you noticed you've gotten taller? And, I heard Granny tell Mr. Canis you were going through puberty."

"What's puberty?"

"There is no way in the world I'm explaining that to you," Sabrina cried. "Drop me, I don't care!"

"This puberty—it must be triggered by some kind of disease. You've given me your cooties, dogface!" Puck's eyes turned bright with flames. "I am the Trickster King. I'm a villain. I am the King of Loafers, the Prince of Low Expectations! The spiritual guide for millions of complainers, criminals, and convicts! Villains do not get married. And they do not get zits. You have poisoned me, Sabrina Grimm. This means war!"

"War?" Sabrina repeated.

Puck swooped down and dropped Sabrina. She landed hard on her behind. He hovered over her, flapping furiously.

"Yes, war! And when I'm done, you'll wish the Scarlet Hand had gotten to you first!" Puck blasted into the sky like a rocket. Within a matter of seconds, he had disappeared from view.

"That went better than I expected," Daphne said.

Uncle Jake staggered around the corner. His arm hung in a sling around his neck. He was pale and seemed to be in a great deal of pain. "Girls, I've been looking everywhere for you. I need your help."

"Uncle Jake, you should be in bed. You need to rest," Daphne scolded.

"I can't. I have to go," he said.

"Go where?" Sabrina asked.

"To rescue Briar Rose."

5

UNCLE JAKE, WE'RE ALL FOR SAVING BRIAR, but leaving the camp is a bad idea right now. We were just out there with Mom and Dad, and we were all almost stomped to death by the Scarlet Hand's goons," Sabrina said.

"Which is exactly why I need to find Briar. Something's wrong. She and the fairy godmothers should have come here already, especially if the town is as bad as everyone is saying."

"Maybe they're leaving her alone," Sabrina said.

"The Scarlet Hand? Leaving my girlfriend alone?" Uncle Jake asked. "Not likely, 'Brina."

He turned and shuffled across the courtyard.

Daphne tried to convince Red to join them, but she was still feeling shy and scared. The sisters left her in her hiding place and hurried to catch up with their uncle. They found him entering Charming's cabin. It was dark and abandoned except for the magic mirrors. Once they entered, Reggie appeared in his reflection.

"Who goes there? Oh, it's you. A little late for scurrying around, don't you think?"

"Sorry if we woke you, Reggie. Go back to sleep," Jake said.

"No worries," he said, then faded away.

Jake lit an oil lamp, and its light cast the cabin in a golden glow. But in the dim light, he looked tired, feverish, and old.

"I have to make sure she gets here safe and sound. We'll take the flying carpet to find her," he continued. "Daphne, you steer. You're better at it than me even when I'm at a hundred percent."

"And what do I do?" Sabrina asked.

"You're going to keep me from falling off the blasted thing."

"I'm in," Daphne said.

Sabrina nodded. "Me too. Should we tell Mom and Dad?"

"Not unless you want them to forbid us from doing it," Daphne said. Then she stepped through the mirror that led to the Hotel of Wonders and vanished.

Sabrina and Uncle Jake followed. With Harry's help, they navigated back to the other portal and found themselves back in the Room of Reflections.

Mirror was there, busy gluing the broken shards from the damaged mirrors to the wall. There were hundreds of pieces, and the light bounced off them in all directions. The girls asked him to retrieve the magic carpet for them, and he put aside his work to get the trolley.

"So, perhaps we should agree on what we're going to tell your father about this plan," Jake said. Mirror had fetched a chair for him, and he slumped in it, looking exhausted.

The girls peered at each other nervously.

"You mean you want us to lie to Dad?" Sabrina asked.

"No! Of course not," Jake said, and then thought for a moment. "Actually, yes. I want all of us to lie to your father. He's being a bit of a jerk."

"You noticed that, too?" Daphne said.

"Hank was always the high-strung one. And very stubborn, too, but he's only trying to protect his family. He's not exactly polite about it, but it's the only way he knows to keep everyone alive. Your grandfather was the same way. I'm more like Mom in a lot of ways—impulsive—"

"NO! You?" Sabrina said with mock surprise.

Uncle Jake laughed. "Guilty as charged."

"Mom and Dad used to be laid-back," Daphne said. "Ever since they woke up, it's been nonstop bickering, with us and each other. If I didn't know better, I would think we woke up the wrong people."

"Not the happily ever after you were hoping for, huh?" Uncle Jake said. "I'm sorry, girls. I think in all the excitement, I've forgotten how important waking them up was to you. And now to have them snapping at everyone—I wish it were different."

Sabrina fought back tears but said nothing. She was glad someone else was disappointed with how the family reunion felt.

Jake closed his eyes and either drifted off to sleep or passed out from the pain. Sabrina and Daphne exchanged a few worried glances but let him rest.

"He's not well, girls," Mirror said when he finally returned with the carpet. "Is this plan of his a life-or-death situation?"

Daphne nodded.

"Then good luck," he said, and then helped them rouse their uncle.

The trio made their way back through the reflection and the Hotel of Wonders, out of Charming's cabin, and into the open courtyard. King Arthur's knights milled about, guarding the camp. A few grew alarmed when the Grimms unrolled the carpet and climbed aboard.

"Charming has ordered that no one leave the camp," Sir Galahad pleaded.

"Tell him we said we're sorry," Daphne said, then turned her attention to the rug. "Up!"

The elegant Persian rug rose high into the air, its tassels rippling in the evening breeze. Sabrina couldn't help admiring the intricate weaving of the carpet, and focusing on it prevented her from getting vertigo as they were propelled skyward. When the rug cleared the high walls of the fort, Daphne instructed it to take them to Briar's coffee shop, Sacred Grounds. At Daphne's instruction, the rug jolted forward, nearly knocking Sabrina over the edge. Her uncle grabbed her hand just in time.

"You're supposed to make sure *I* don't fall off," he reminded her.

"Sorry," she said. "This thing really needs seat belts."

"It's easier if you relax. It can sense your stress. Just sit down and try to enjoy the ride," Daphne explained over the wind. Sabrina tried to take her advice and found she was right. The more relaxed she was, the better the ride, but it wasn't easy. The quarter moon above did little to illuminate the forest below, so flying above it was like sailing over a black abyss. Sabrina worried about what might be lurking among the trees, waiting to attack. She imagined the hideous roar of the Jabberwocky or a hobgoblin.

Uncle Jake seemed to read her mind. "You forget that under all his arrogance the prince is brilliant. I doubt that those hobgoblins could ever find the camp again. Still, it's good that Snow is training some of the refugees. Charming should make it mandatory."

"You think they'll need to fight back against the Hand?" Daphne asked.

"Absolutely," Uncle Jake replied. "Will they win? It's hard to say. They're completely outnumbered. And even if they do manage to raise an army, it will consist of elderly witches, gentle animals, and princesses. Only a few of them have any real fighting experience."

"So, if the odds are against the camp, why are we going to find Briar and bring her back there?"

"Because she can help. She's smart," Jake said. Briar Rose was the basis for the famous story of Sleeping Beauty, but unlike a lot of the royalty Sabrina had met, she was also a resourceful woman. Sabrina thought of Briar, Snow White, and Granny Relda as role models.

"Plus, her fairy godmothers are a force to be reckoned with," he continued.

"We'll find her," Sabrina promised.

Uncle Jake nodded.

Daphne steered the rug westward. "We're coming up on the farms. Oh, no! Look!"

Sabrina expected to see huge fields of corn and wheat, neatly planted in rows, and maybe the occasional cow mooing at the moon, but what they found was unrecognizable. Much of Ferryport Landing's farmland was in ruins. The little houses that freckled the fields were ablaze.

"The Scarlet Hand has been here," Uncle Jake said gravely. "Recently."

"But aren't these Everafter farms?" Daphne asked. "Why burn them?"

"The owners must have resisted joining the Master," Uncle Jake said, as his jaw stiffened. "Can you make this thing go faster?"

Daphne nodded and spoke a few words of encouragement to the carpet. It picked up speed, now streaking across the sky. Uncle Jake nearly fell over the side, but this time Sabrina did her job and kept him upright. Soon, the farms of Ferryport Landing were behind them and the town proper was just ahead.

Daphne slowed the carpet and lowered it until they were hovering a few feet above the ground on Main Street. Once there, the trio absorbed the shocking scene before them. Stores were gutted, their contents spilling onto the street. Old King Cole's restaurant was nothing but a burned-out shell, as was the Blue Plate Special diner. Cars lay on their backs like dead beetles. Bicycles were scattered in the middle of the street, bent beyond repair. The wire that held the town's one and only traffic light had snapped, and the light lay shattered on the road.

"Get this thing to the coffee shop, now!" Uncle Jake blurted out.

The rug didn't wait for Daphne's command. It zipped down the street toward the little shop. But, when they arrived, they found Sacred Grounds destroyed. The windows were black with soot. The roof had collapsed. The only thing untouched by the flames was the hand-painted sign that once hung over the door. It now lay on the ground. A red handprint covered the name.

Despite his injury, Uncle Jake leaped off the rug before it came to a full stop. He rushed to the shop and threw open the door. A blast of still-smoldering fire exploded out, and Uncle Jake fell backward. The girls rushed to his side and helped him to his feet.

Uncle Jake groaned. "I fell on my shoulder."

"You can't go in there," Sabrina said, snatching him by the hand.

"I have to," he protested, trying to pull away.

"Looking for your sweetheart, Jake?" a voice called out from behind them. When the Grimms spun around, they found Sheriff Nottingham glowering behind them. The flames from the building illuminated his face and exaggerated his scar. The red handprint on his chest held an eerie glow.

"Where is she, Nottingham?" Jake demanded.

"She's dead. Or she will be soon," the sheriff said, his white teeth flashing.

Jake charged the sheriff and swung wildly. Before the villain could pull out his dagger, Jake's fist slammed into his cheek. Nottingham howled and collapsed to the ground. Bewildered, he grasped for his dagger, but Jake didn't give him a chance to use it. His hands went into a coat pocket, and, in a flash, the sheriff was enclosed in a perfect green bubble. When Jake lifted his hand, the bubble and its prisoner rose as well. Nottingham kicked and fought like an angry marionette, but he was completely helpless.

"You've made a terrible mistake, Grimm," the sheriff shouted.

"The mistake is yours, Nottingham. You think that I am good-natured like my mother or my father. But you've got me all wrong."

"Is that so? Then who are you, Jacob?" Nottingham sneered.

"A man who will kill to protect the people he loves."

Nottingham paled.

"Where is she?" Jake pressed.

Nottingham shook his head.

Jake swung his arm around, and the bubble followed his every move. He slammed it into an abandoned building, and Nottingham let out a pained groan. Jake aimed the bubble at a building across the street, with similar results. When he returned the bubble to the middle of the street, the sheriff scampered to his feet. His nose was covered in blood.

"Tell me, Nottingham!" Jake shouted.

"Heart has her home surrounded," the sheriff groaned. "Her fairy godmothers are holding them off, but they can't last forever. She's probably already dead."

A long, ropelike stem appeared at the top of the bubble. It wrapped itself around a streetlight, and the sheriff hung there like an evil Christmas ornament.

"You better hope not. I'm going after her, Nottingham," Uncle Jake growled. "If a single hair on her head has been harmed, I'll come back for you."

He stepped onto the flying carpet, and the girls followed. Once they were in the air, Uncle Jake collapsed. Sweat poured down his forehead, and he looked ashen.

"Remind me to punch people with my good arm," he said weakly, and then passed out.

"Do you think he meant it?" Daphne asked. "Do you really think he'd kill Nottingham?"

Sabrina stared at her uncle. It was like she was seeing him for the first time. Maybe he was capable of murder, or maybe it was all talk. She just couldn't be sure.

"What do we do now?" Daphne asked.

"The smartest thing would be to bring Uncle Jake back to the camp to get some rest, but—"

"But?"

"But Briar is in trouble."

"She needs our help."

"Daphne, we're just a couple of kids. Can we stop an entire mob by ourselves? I don't think he's going to wake up anytime soon," Sabrina said, nudging Uncle Jake.

Daphne dug through Uncle Jake's jacket pockets and pulled out a handful of trinkets. "We're a couple of kids with magic weapons."

"Do you know how to use any of those?" Sabrina asked.

Daphne shrugged and shoved the enchanted objects into her own pockets. "How hard could it be?"

There was real confidence in Daphne's eyes. Dad might treat her like a baby, but Sabrina knew Daphne was more courageous than most adults.

"It's your call, then," Sabrina offered.

"Really?"

Sabrina nodded. "I should have said this a long time ago. I have more faith in you than anyone else I know."

Daphne smiled and hugged her sister. "I'm still mad at you."

"I know."

"Carpet," Daphne commanded, "take us to Briar Rose's house, and step on it."

Daphne gave the carpet instructions while Sabrina attended to her uncle. Jake looked pale and vulnerable in the night sky, his skin sallow.

Daphne brought the carpet to a slow crawl as they approached Briar's home. Briar lived in a sturdy Victorian, painted sea green, with a round column on each side of the door and a stained-glass rose window set into the second story. Jake had told them about Briar's dozens of rosebushes, and he wasn't exaggerating. The perimeter of the house was lined with the beautiful flowering plants: reds, whites, and yellows.

Unfortunately, many of the bushes had been trampled by the horde of Everafters surrounding the house. The mob was made up of goblins, witches, knights, and a near-giant—a twenty-foot-tall man carrying an ax nearly that long. He wore a flannel shirt, a big, bushy beard, and a red handprint on his enormous chest. Paul Bunyan had joined the Scarlet Hand.

"Look who's leading the pack," Daphne said, pointing to a familiar woman in a red dress. Mayor Heart was barking orders through her megaphone.

"Do you think Briar is still alive?" Daphne asked, taking the magical trinkets out of her pocket to give them another look.

"I hope so. At least we know her fairy godmothers are going strong," Sabrina said, pointing toward the house.

A green blast of magic shot out of an open window and hit a goblin. His fierce metal armor suddenly transformed into an elaborate silk gown. The goblin tripped over his hoop skirt and tumbled onto his back, unable to right himself.

Another blast came from the window and nailed a troll, who found himself sporting a feathery headdress and high heels, like a Las Vegas showgirl. He cried indignantly and shook a mace at the house.

"Let's go give them some help," Daphne said, urging the carpet forward. Soon they were barreling into the midst of the Scarlet Hand's army. When the villains noticed the flying carpet, they turned their attention to the girls. Swords slashed and wands launched deadly spells. But the nimble carpet banked and weaved expertly through the angry crowd, and the Grimms remained unscathed.

"Uh, maybe it's time to use one of those magic doohickeys?" Sabrina asked.

"I'm working on it," Daphne said. She slipped on a huge ring with a stone scorpion set inside an emerald and waved it around. "Abracadabra!"

The ring popped and sparked like metal in the microwave, but it didn't seem to do anything helpful. Daphne shrugged and exchanged it for a second ring, this one with a small tooth embedded in amber. "Gimme some magic!"

This time, nothing happened—not even a spark.

Sabrina was starting to worry, especially when the carpet hovered too close to an angry knight. He swung his sword wildly, nearly cutting the carpet, and the sisters, in two. Sabrina kicked him in the helmet. His visor came down over his face, and he staggered into a rosebush, where the vines held him fast.

The carpet veered away from the mob. Sabrina turned to her sister, who was trying out one of three magic wands. It was made of little red jewels fused together like a long stick of rock candy.

"Any luck?" Sabrina asked. "That knight almost gave me a haircut."

"Hold your horses," Daphne said. She waved the wand, and it started to glow. "Now we're talking."

"What does it do?" Sabrina asked.

Daphne shrugged. "Your guess is as good as mine."

She waved it around some more, but nothing happened.

Daphne frowned. "Set something on fire!" she begged.

Nothing.

"Freeze the bad guys!"

Zilch.

"Shoot electricity!"

Nada.

Daphne huffed. "This thing is for the birds."

All of a sudden, a flash of light blinded Sabrina.

"No way!" Daphne exclaimed, her eyes widening with surprise.

"What?"

"OK, don't be mad. I didn't know it would do that," Daphne said.

"WHAT?"

"Take a look at your back," Daphne muttered.

Sabrina peeked over her shoulder and stifled a scream. On her back was a set of huge white wings. The feathers fluttered in the wind, and when she tensed up, they flapped.

"Oh, no!" she cried. "Change me back. I can't go through life with wings!"

"It's not the wings that're the problem," Daphne said. "It's the beak."

Sabrina crossed her eyes to find a hard, golden beak with a hooked tip. She shrieked, but what came out sounded more like a squawk. "Fix me!"

Mayor Heart's voice ripped through the air. "Ignore the children. Attack the house until Briar and her traitorous fairies are dead! Our backup can handle the Grimms."

"Backup? I don't like the sound of that," Daphne said, steering the rug to avoid a flying spear. "I wonder who it is."

"Who cares about the backup? I look like Big Bird!" Sabrina complained.

"OK! OK!" Daphne cried. She flicked the wand at Sabrina and said, "Change her back!" But nothing happened. "OK, let's not panic," she reassured her sister.

"'Let's not panic'?" Sabrina cried. "I'm starting to get a craving for worms. It's definitely time to panic."

Daphne steered the carpet low over the crowd. With one hand, she removed her sneaker and used it wallop a few heads. Clearly, she'd abandoned magical solutions after the latest mishap.

"I realize this is inconvenient, but you need to focus. We're here to rescue Briar Rose."

"Excuse me if I'm a little distracted—*honk*!" Sabrina was horrified by the sound she made. "Did I—?"

"Yeah . . . you honked," Daphne confirmed with a guilty grimace. She smacked a few more trolls with her shoe. "Think on the bright side. At least Puck isn't here. He'd never let you forget it."

Uncle Jake groaned and opened his eyes slowly. When he saw Sabrina, he shoved her off the rug in midair with a "Shooo!"

"NO!" Sabrina cried, plummeting toward the ground. In desperation, she flapped her wings as hard as she could, and it seemed to slow her fall. Unfortunately, she was so busy concentrating on staying aloft that she forgot to watch where she was going. She sailed through an open window and crashed to the floor.

She scrambled to her feet and called out for Briar Rose. Instead, she found Briar's two fairy godmothers, wands drawn. Buzzflower and Mallobarb were stout, intimidating women. Their dark, menacing eyes told her that she better not move a muscle—or a feather.

"We're giving you three seconds to take your filthy, traitorous bottom out of here, goose," Mallobarb threatened.

"And tell the rest of the Scarlet Hand they're going to have to send a lot more than a bird if they want take us down," Buzzflower added.

"I'm not a goose!" Sabrina cried.

"Well, you aren't a Bengal tiger," said Mallobarb.

"I'm Sabrina Grimm!" she honked. "I'm here to rescue you."

The fairy godmothers looked at each other in disbelief, then back at Sabrina.

"Really?"

"Listen, my uncle is here. And my sister, too."

"Jake is here?" Buzzflower asked.

"He is?" a voice called from down the hall. A moment later Briar Rose raced into the room, wielding a baseball bat.

Sabrina pointed out the window with her wing just as the flying carpet zipped past.

"So, what's the plan?" Buzzflower asked.

"Yeah . . . a plan. We kind of got sidetracked when my sister turned me into a bird," Sabrina admitted.

"Great," Mallobarb said sarcastically. "Jacob Grimm is quite a catch, Briar."

"What we need is a distraction," Briar said, ignoring the insult. "If we can get the mob outside to focus on something other than the house, we can fly out of here ourselves."

"Sounds good to me," Sabrina said. "What do you have in mind?"

"I think a giant goose might confuse them for a bit," Buzzflower said.

"You want me to fly out the window and let them shoot at me?"

The fairy godmothers nodded.

"I could be killed!"

The fairy godmothers nodded again.

"No," Briar said. "That's too dangerous. If something were to happen to Sabrina, I could never live with myself."

"What choice do we have?" Mallobarb said.

Sabrina peered out the window. Her sister was having little success.

"OK, I'll do it, but I've only been a bird for five minutes. I haven't quite figured out flying yet. If I manage to stay in the air, you have to act fast. Get out of the house as soon as you can."

"And then what?" Buzzflower asked.

"Prince Charming and Mr. Canis have built a camp. We'll take you there," Sabrina said.

"Good luck," Briar said.

"Here goes nothing!" Sabrina cried as she leaped out the window, flapping her wings as hard as she could.

Her sudden appearance drew the full ferocity of the crowd. Dozens of arrows, magical blasts, and even one electronic megaphone rocketed toward her. She dodged left and right, until a spear clipped her tail feathers. It startled her, and she fell right onto a hobgoblin's head. The creature tried to clobber her, but she scampered off and landed on another. She quickly leaped from one hobgoblin to the next before landing on the beehive hairdo of the Queen of Hearts herself. Heart screamed and slapped at the goose. Sabrina pecked at the mayor's hands viciously before springing into the air. She flapped wildly and, much to her surprise, stayed aloft. She flew away from the mob and joined Daphne and Uncle Jake back beside the carpet.

When she looked back toward the house, she spotted Buzz-flower and Mallobarb carrying Briar Rose out of the window and through the air, a stream of magical dust floating behind them. They fled toward the woods. The trio followed but soon lost them in the thick of the trees.

Sabrina heard Mayor Heart commanding her troops. "Don't follow the traitors. We'll let the pack handle them."

"'The pack'? What's 'the pack'?" Daphne asked.

Before anyone could hazard a guess, a crashing sound came from deep within the trees, and then a creature as big as a jumbo jet flew overhead. It had red wings and a long tail. Sabrina knew anything that big and fast couldn't be good news. Worse still, it was not alone. A second creature appeared. This one was green and covered in black spikes.

"There's another one!" Daphne cried, pointing to a third creature. This one was purple with a white snout. Fire blasted out of its nostrils and lit up the sky.

"Dragons!" Uncle Jake cried. "We need to catch up with Briar and the fairies *now*!"

"Dragons, your target and her cohorts have fled into the woods," the mayor bellowed. "Retrieve them any way you can, dead or alive."

The creatures flew deeper into the forest with amazing speed. They cleared huge swaths of trees with fiery blasts, trying to get a glimpse of their prey.

Daphne commanded the carpet to chase after the dragons. Sabrina tilted her wings and followed, still surprised she could fly at all. If she hadn't been so terrified, she might have enjoyed it. But flying through the trees was treacherous. Several branches scraped her soft belly, and a few lashed her face. As the trees got denser, even the carpet couldn't navigate around them without a few scrapes. Thankfully, Sabrina soon spotted Briar and her fairy godmothers, racing on foot through the brambles below.

"Carpet, down!" Uncle Jake shouted. A moment later, they were hovering in Briar's path.

"Get on," Uncle Jake said. "They've sent dragons after you."

"Dragons!" Briar cried. "Where did they get dragons?"

"Briar, you go with them. We'll have a better chance of escaping by air," Buzzflower said.

"She's right," Mallobarb added, taking out her wand. "And they might find we're a little harder to kill, too."

Briar climbed up onto the rug. Jake clung to her and kissed her deeply.

"I don't know what I'd do if I lost you," he said.

"It looks like I almost lost *you*," she said, eyeing his wounded shoulder. "What happened?"

"It's nothing," he said, quickly. "Daphne, get us back to the camp."

Sabrina turned to the fairy godmothers. "If you lose us, it's at the farthest edge of the barrier."

At that moment the purple dragon's head dipped down through the trees. The creature studied the group with its bulging yellow eyes.

"Daphne! Go!" Uncle Jake begged.

"C'mon, rug!" Daphne shouted, and the carpet shot skyward, narrowly missing the dragon's fiery breath.

Sabrina followed as best she could, flapping hard to fly higher and higher. When she felt out of danger, she moved in a wide circle above the forest. Daphne, Jake, and Briar Rose were speeding along below, and the two fairy godmothers were rapidly firing magical attacks at the dragons.

Unfortunately, Sabrina's feeling of security was short-lived. She saw the red dragon rising from the ground like a missile, its deadly mouth open wide. She swooped suddenly to the left, dodging its jaws as they clamped down just inches from her. The creature's gnashing teeth sounded like a car crash.

She flew to the left, then to the right. The monster's breath scorched her tail feathers. No matter where she went, it chased her. Even when she dropped back into the trees, the dragon smashed through them, pulverizing huge oaks and giant maples as easily a child running through tall grass.

Sabrina knew she couldn't outrun it for long—she was already tired, and the tree limbs kept clipping her wings, making it impossible to coast on the breeze. When a stiff limb caught her across the chest, she tumbled to the ground. The fall shook her, but she staggered to her feet and hopped along the forest floor.

The red dragon crashed to the ground, blocking her path. Its head dipped low to scrutinize her. The creature let out a satisfied chuckle. It reared back, inhaling deeply into its mouth and nose, apparently preparing to blast Sabrina. She knew there was nothing she could do to escape, and she braced herself for death.

"Run, child," a voice called from above. Sabrina looked up to see Buzzflower floating above the dragon's head. She waved her wand at the creature, and a bolt of blue energy exploded into the dragon's chest. The dragon screeched and fell backward, landing with a loud thud.

Sabrina turned and fled as fast as her legs would allow, until she heard a horrible roar. She turned to see flames rising up into the trees. Had Buzzflower been hit? There was no way to know, but Sabrina feared the worst. She heard more angry roars, saw more fiery blasts, and suddenly the dragon was in front of her again.

"Fine! You want to kill me, I'm right here!" Sabrina shouted. "But don't be too proud of yourself, lizard face. I'm weakened by this stupid spell. If I was my normal self, you would never stand a chance against me."

"You speak gibberish, child," the dragon said. Its voice was like a thousand volcanoes exploding at once.

Child? How did it know she was a child? She looked down, wondering if he could see through her magical transformation, and saw that her feathers were gone. Her wings had vanished. Even the hard yellow beak was nowhere to be found. The magic had worn off.

"Great," she grumbled. "It wears off just in time for me to be roasted like a marshmallow."

"Not tonight, big sis!"

Suddenly, Daphne hoisted Sabrina up onto the flying carpet. They darted away, the monster roaring in frustration.

"See? I told you it was temporary!" Daphne said.

"You did not," Sabrina challenged, trying to get her bearings.

"Well, I meant to," Daphne said. She turned to Briar Rose and Uncle Jake. "Dudes, can we slow down on the kissing? We need all the magic we can get. What do you have in that jacket that fights dragons?"

"Preferably something with instructions," Sabrina added.

Uncle Jake pulled out vials of strange liquids, weird rings and amulets, and even a smelly fur hat. He laid them all on the rug for Daphne and Sabrina to examine.

"It's not much, ladies, except maybe this will help," he said, choosing a small black coin from the pile. He rubbed his hand over it for a moment, and it began to spin.

"What is it?" Daphne asked.

"You'll see," Jake said.

The dragon brushed the rug, causing them to spiral out of control. In the collision, Jake fell hard onto his shoulder. He let out a howl and then passed out from the pain.

"Oh, Jake," Briar cried, as she cradled his head in her lap.

"There's got to be something else in that jacket," Sabrina said. "Briar, help me search."

They shoved their hands into as many pockets as they could until Briar found a small felt-covered box.

"What's that?" Sabrina asked.

Briar opened it. Inside was a bright diamond ring. The stone was emerald-cut and mounted on a platinum band.

"Is that—" Daphne gasped as she watched Briar Rose slip it onto her ring finger. Though she was laughing and smiling widely, Briar's cheeks were wet with tears.

"YES!" she cried. "Yes, I will marry you, Jacob Grimm."

"You might want to wait until he's awake," Sabrina said, with a smile.

"You may be right." Briar giggled and put the ring away.

Mallobarb joined them, flying alongside the carpet. "My wand has almost no effect on the dragons now," she said. "It's only making them angrier."

"Where's the coin?" Daphne begged.

Sabrina found it lying beside her uncle's hand. She grabbed it and quickly passed it to her sister. Daphne flipped it over several times and then rubbed her hand over it, just as Uncle Jake had done. Soon, it was spinning faster and faster.

When the green dragon got close enough, Daphne tossed the coin directly at it, where it landed in its gaping maw. Bolts of lightning sparked out from inside its jaws and erupted out of its fat belly. The dragon fell out of the sky, but before it hit the ground, it exploded.

"Gross," Sabrina said. "Next time, warn a person before you blow a dragon up in front of her. I'm going to have nightmares until I'm a hundred years old."

"Sorry," Daphne said. "I didn't know it was going to do that, either. Now for the other two."

"Shouldn't we just try to outrun them?" Sabrina asked.

"You can't outrun a dragon, 'Brina," Uncle Jake said, stirring. "I've tried."

The purple dragon had been circling above them but now dove like a kamikaze pilot. The carpet easily dodged its attack, but the monster was not discouraged. It looped around to attack again. Once again, the carpet swerved to safety.

"Land this thing," Uncle Jake suggested. "We won't have a chance if we stay in the air."

Daphne did as she was told, landing in a nearby clearing, where they were joined by Mallobarb and Buzzflower. Uncle Jake struggled to his feet and shooed everyone from the rug. He begged the fairy godmothers to help find shelter for the others.

"Use whatever protection spells you know," he commanded.

The fairy godmothers didn't like Uncle Jake's demanding tone. They frowned, but Briar spoke up. "Just this once—don't argue. He's trying to help."

Mallobarb forced a smile and led the group toward the safety of the trees just as the purple dragon landed hard on the ground in front of Uncle Jake. Jake didn't even flinch. In fact, he smiled.

"You are either brave or stupid," the dragon croaked.

"Maybe a little bit of both," Uncle Jake replied. "In fact, many of your kind would say the same of you for challenging Jake Grimm. But I don't expect you to know who I am. I suppose you don't get out of town very often."

"I'll consider myself warned, human, and I will return the favor. I'm about to roast your bones. You should run."

"No need," Jake said as he dug into his pockets. "I happen to have the Amulet of Roona."

"Liar," the dragon growled.

"No. It's right here," he said, fumbling nervously.

Sabrina pointed to the handful of rings and necklaces Daphne held. "Could one of those be the Amulet of Roona?"

Daphne cringed. "Uh, Uncle Jake, what does the Amulet of Roona look like?"

"It's a black necklace with a silver crescent moon."

Daphne sorted frantically through the items she'd taken from Jake's pockets. She held up a necklace that looked exactly like the one her uncle described. "Um, is this it?"

"Fudge."

The dragon chuckled and took a deep breath. Sabrina could hear the flames building inside its throat.

Uncle Jake shoved his hands into another pocket, but it was too late. The dragon blasted him, and the flames engulfed his entire body. His body darkened until it looked like a piece of charcoal, his features reduced to those of a volcanic rock. After what felt like minutes, the fire was gone. The forest was full of smoke and cinders that burned Sabrina's eyes.

"No!" Briar cried. Her fairy godmothers tried to hold her back, but she broke free and ran to Jake's charred body, which was frozen in place like a statue.

Tears spilled from Sabrina's eyes. Daphne was in hysterics, sobbing and trembling. Briar collapsed. Mallobarb attended to her, but she was just as shaken, her face cracked and confused.

"We should go," Mallobarb said to Sabrina. "The beast will turn on us."

Sabrina shook her head. If they wanted her to leave, then they would have to drag her away. She would fight the dragon with her bare hands now. Briar seemed to feel the same way. The princess lunged at the monster, kicking and punching at its huge, taloned feet. The dragon looked down at her as if she were some minor annoyance—like an ant invading its lunch—then swatted her away. Briar slammed into a tree. There was a sickly crack, and she collapsed to the ground.

"Briar!" Buzzflower cried, rushing to her side.

"Who's next?" the creature hissed.

Sabrina braced herself for death, but something stole the monster's attention away. Something was happening to Uncle Jake's body. The smoldering black shell that covered him split. Pieces of it fell off and crumbled to dust on the ground. Inside, completely unharmed, was her uncle, and in his hand was a dark-green crystal, glowing like a small star.

"Luckily, I always keep a spare invulnerability crystal on me, in case of emergencies," he said, then reached, once again, into one of his pockets. From it, he pulled an impossibly long broadsword. It was now clear to Sabrina that his jacket was just as magical as the things he stored inside it. In one quick motion, he lunged at the dragon, shoved the sword under its chin, and easily sliced through the creature's steel-strong skin. The dragon let out a muffled cry and then, with a ground-shaking thud, fell over dead.

High above, the red dragon roared in rage.

"You want some?" Uncle Jake laughed. The dragon flew off. "That's what I thought, punk!"

"Jacob," Buzzflower said to get his attention.

Jake turned to her and saw his fallen girlfriend. He raced to her side and cradled her in his arms.

"What happened?" Uncle Jake cried.

"The dragon—" Sabrina started, but it was all she could muster before tears took over.

"Briar? Briar, honey. Wake up for me," Jake begged. "We've got to get her back to the camp. Nurse Sprat can help. She's got medicines, and I've got—"

"She's gone, Jacob," Mallobarb said.

Uncle Jake buried his face in Briar's hair and he wept. "No, no, no."

Sabrina and Daphne stood on the edge of the clearing. For the first time in days, they hugged each other like sisters.

6

THE SISTERS, THEIR PARENTS, AND GRANNY
Relda stood in the huge crowd gathered around a vacant
space in the camp, now designated as a cemetery. Mr.
Canis stood shoulder to shoulder with Robin Hood and Prince
Charming. The three men somberly gazed down at the crude casket Geppetto had built for Briar. Pinocchio had helped carry it to
the plot where her body would rest. Red Riding Hood placed a
bouquet of wildflowers she had gathered along the camp's walls in
Briar's hands. Briar still looked beautiful, as if she were once again
the sleeping princess from the storybooks.

Uncle Jake stood with Mallobarb and Buzzflower. The fairy
godmothers sobbed, while Jake stood still and silent. His love for
Briar, though new, was well-known throughout the town, and the
refugees felt his heartbreak.

Daphne was inconsolable. She clung to her mother, weeping.

Elvis sat next to her, licking her wet cheeks. Sabrina wanted to be strong for her sister but choked back her own sobs.

"Today is a dark day for us," Prince Charming said as he stepped before the grave. "We have lost one of our own and one of our most precious. Like many of us, Briar Rose came to America aboard the *New Beginning*, searching for a new life. She left a kingdom and a family behind, but she brought with her two fairy godmothers, Mallobarb and Buzzflower, who have been by her side for nearly seven hundred years. They have kept Briar safe from wicked witches and from a foolish husband."

The crowd chuckled. It was rare for Charming to speak of his relationship with Briar.

"Sadly, the reign of terror that has affected all of our lives has taken its first victim. Briar was killed by one of the Master's dragons, and—"

"They have a dragon?!" Little Boy Blue cried. The crowd fell into fearful chaos, but Robin Hood begged everyone to remain calm.

"They have more than one," Charming said. "Jacob Grimm managed to kill two and chased off a third. There could be even more."

"Where did they come from?" Morgan le Fay asked. "I thought the Grimms had all the dragon eggs."

"We have those that we were given to look after," Granny

said. "But not everyone was willing to part with their enchanted possessions, and my family has never forced them to."

Charming raised his hand for the crowd's attention. "We can discuss this issue later. Now, I would like to let the people who knew Briar Rose the best speak about her," Charming said. "Starting with myself. I found Briar's castle centuries ago, wrapped in a thorn hedge. My youthful zeal for exploration and treasure drove me to cut through it, but I didn't know the actual treasure I would find. Briar was one of the most beautiful women I had ever met. But her truest beauty was internal. She was, above all, kind and patient, thoughtful and encouraging. She could be smart, funny, and wise. I was not the husband I should have been to her. My heart was somewhere else, and she knew it even better than I did. She set me free. She never held a grudge. She was gracious about the end of our marriage and moved on to a new, happy life. I was not a good man when I met her, but I am all the better for having known her. I count myself as one of the luckiest people in the world for having shared a life with her. I will miss you, Briar." Charming welled up but pulled himself together. "Now, I'd like to ask Mallobarb and Buzzflower to speak."

The fairy godmothers stepped forward and lifted their sad faces to the crowd. "Briar was a brave woman. She was also strong, stubborn, and opinionated . . . but brave," Mallobarb said, holding back tears.

"She faced many obstacles in her life—evil witches, monsters, heartbreak—all with determination and a smile . . . and somehow she always came out on top," Buzzflower said. "Her death was tragic, but it comes as no surprise to us that she died for someone she truly loved. I will miss her humor, her strong sense of right and wrong, and her companionship. Though my sister and I helped raise her, I feel we learned more from her than she ever learned from us. Good-bye, my sweet rose." She blew a kiss to the casket.

"Jacob?" Charming called.

Uncle Jake stepped forward. He turned to the Everafters as if about to say something about the woman he loved. But, instead, he reached into his pocket and took out the box that held her engagement ring. He slipped the ring onto Briar Rose's finger, leaned over, and kissed her on the lips. Then, Jake rejoined the crowd.

Charming stepped forward once more. "Death has come to our door. Briar was our first casualty. I know what you are thinking: *Casualty* is a word people use for death in the midst of war. And we are at war, even if you have chosen not to fight with us. The battle is at our door, and if we stand idly by, we may as well dig our own graves."

Mr. Seven appeared with a shovel on his shoulder. "Who wants to dig their own grave?" the prince asked.

The crowd eyed the shovel as if it were a scorpion preparing to strike.

"These are your choices. Join Sleeping Beauty, or fight."

Sabrina scanned the crowd. There, she saw so many familiar faces—Snow White, Friar Tuck, Puss in Boots, Morgan le Fay, Old King Cole, Frau Pfefferkuchenhaus, Rip Van Winkle, Sawhorse, the Scarecrow, the Pied Piper and his son, Wendell, Lancelot, Cinderella and her husband, Tom, and Jack Pumpkinhead. There were Munchkins and Lilliputians, Yahoos and shoe elves. There were brutish creatures like the blacksmith troll and a cyclops, but also delicate beauties like Little Bo Peep and her flock of sheep. There were also many Everafters Sabrina didn't know and had never seen before that day.

"Why should we trust you, Charming?" Ichabod Crane asked from the middle of the crowd.

"Weren't you yourself a member of the Scarlet Hand? How do we know this isn't some trap?" a duckling quacked.

"Let me explain," Charming said fiercely. The crowd erupted into shouts and arguments, but the noise stopped when Mr. Canis stepped forward.

"Charming's words are true, but since you need to hear it from someone else, hear it from me. The war is coming. If we fight, many of us will die. If we don't, then *all* of us will die. We have a chance to beat them back, but we have to prepare this camp."

Uncle Jake stepped forward. "I will fight."

Henry gasped. "Jake, no!"

"Thank you, Jacob," Charming said, then turned back to the crowd. "Is there no one else? A human has stepped forward to fight for you! A human!"

Mallobarb and Buzzflower joined him. "We will fight."

Mr. Seven raised the shovel. "I will fight."

Morgan le Fay stepped up next to Seven and looked down at him. "I will fight, too."

The little man smiled and gave her hand a squeeze.

"Anyone else?" Charming called.

Poppa, Momma, and Baby Bear roared. Puss in Boots joined the group. Beauty and her beastly daughter, Natalie, were next, then former deputies Mr. Boarman and Mr. Swineheart. The bridge troll and Rip Van Winkle stepped forward, followed by the Munchkins, then the Winkies, then the Gillikins. The Lilliputians, the Mouse King and his royal subjects, several Houyhnhnms, a huge contingent of knights, princes, princesses, and witches, and finally Jack Pumpkinhead all joined.

"I will fight," they said in unison.

The last refugee was Ichabod Crane, who frowned before reluctantly stepping forward himself. "Fine, but if I see that one of those Scarlet Hand thugs is missing a head, I'm deserting."

The crowd roared and shook their fists in the air.

Charming turned to his team. Mr. Seven, Robin Hood, Snow White, and Mr. Canis nodded in approval, and he nodded back.

Then he removed his purple suit jacket and tossed it aside. He took the shovel from Seven and began to dig Briar's grave. Uncle Jake stopped him and held out his hand. Charming nodded respectfully, passed Jake the shovel, and stepped aside.

Overhead, rain clouds opened, soaking the camp. The refugees drifted away, but Sabrina and her family stayed to watch Jake dig. When the hole was deep enough, he gave his love one final kiss, then closed the casket's heavy lid. Charming and Henry helped Jake lower the box into the grave and stood by as he filled the hole with dirt. When Briar was buried, Mallobarb and Buzzflower planted a single seed on top of the plot. Moments later, fed by rainwater and magic, a rosebush sprouted and grew in its spot.

The next morning, Camp Charming became Fort Charming. Sabrina was surrounded by a flurry of fight training, forging, and construction. Mr. Boarman and Mr. Swineheart directed the work, and, with the help of some witches and wizards, the fort soon doubled in size. Teams of volunteers built lookout towers, fortifying them with cannons, while others built a catapult big enough to hurl a pickup truck over the walls.

Everyone volunteered for Snow White's army, and she trained them in hand-to-hand combat. Under her command, Everafters of all shapes and sizes ran drills, rappelled down the tall fort walls, and—Snow's favorite—dropped at a moment's notice for

muscle-straining pushups. It was very strange to see the ancient Frau Pfefferkuchenhaus crawling on her belly beneath barbed wire.

Henry continued to search for a way out of the town, and Veronica continued to try to convince him to stay. As they bickered, the girls were left to their own devices. They searched for some way to be useful. They came across Pinocchio sitting under an oak tree and carving a dozen small wooden heads with a sharp knife. His work was highly detailed, and his mastery of the blade was incredible.

"You're making puppets," Daphne said, picking up one of the heads and examining it.

"They are called marionettes," Pinocchio said.

"What's the difference?" Daphne asked.

"A marionette is a wooden figure with limbs attached to strings, and someone manipulates the strings to make it move," Sabrina explained.

"And that's not a puppet?" Daphne asked.

Pinocchio bristled at the little girl's confusion. "No, a puppet has someone's hand up its bum. A marionette can walk, dance, and perform in any way its master desires."

"And now you're making them, just like your father," Sabrina said, continuing to admire his work.

Pinocchio nodded. "It's a skill I've been working on for some time. The secret is to use the right wood. If it's too hard, it's impossible to carve, but if it's too soft, then the whole piece can fall apart in your hands. It took me forever to find the right wood, but now that I have, I carry it with me."

"Must get heavy," Sabrina said, noticing the huge bag the boy had brought with him to the camp.

"A tad," the boy said as if slightly annoyed, then changed the subject. "My condolences for your loss."

Sabrina thanked him and blinked back tears. "She was the best."

"She seems to have been quite an exceptional woman and an asset to the Everafter community."

Sabrina nodded, though she was unnerved by Pinocchio's manner of speaking. She couldn't get used to his sophisticated vocabulary.

Before she could respond, Goldilocks appeared. "Girls, your grandmother would like to see you in Charming's cabin."

The girls said good-bye to Pinocchio. They crossed the fort to Charming's cabin, where they found their father and grandmother in the midst of a heated argument.

"If he does it again, I'll knock him out," Henry said. "None of you have a right to sneak my children out in the middle of the night to fight dragons."

"Good heavens," Granny Relda said. "Your brother didn't sneak them out to fight dragons. I'm sure he had no idea they would run into trouble."

"We're lucky *any* of them came back alive," Henry snapped.

"Henry!" Veronica cried. "Lower your voice. He might hear you."

"I'm sorry, but this is not OK. If he needed to go after Briar, he shouldn't have turned to two children for help."

Granny stepped forward. "Henry, I'm not happy about it either, but the girls are very capable. Why, Sabrina killed a giant once."

"She nearly kills me every time she looks at me." Puck snickered as he strolled into the cabin. He was filthy from head to toe, as though he had spent the morning playing in a toxic waste dump. "What's all the hubbub about?"

Henry ignored him. "They're my children, Mom."

"Hello?" Veronica interrupted.

Henry scowled. "They're not sidekicks. They're not personal flying-carpet chauffeurs. They're not junior detectives or monster-fighters in training. They're little girls."

"Little girls?!" the sisters said at once.

Henry ignored them, too. "If any of you tries to involve them in another stupid scheme, I will personally wring your neck," Henry threatened.

Just then, Uncle Jake entered the cabin. He said nothing, even though he definitely heard the shouting. He sat in a chair by the window and looked out at the sky. Mr. Canis followed, and, much to the shock of Sabrina and Daphne, Little Red Riding Hood was with him.

"Now that everyone is here, we need to have a family meeting," announced Mr. Canis.

"Since when do we have family meetings?" Sabrina asked.

"Since now," Henry said.

Red turned to leave.

"Where are you going, *liebling*?" Granny asked.

"I'm not a member of your family," Red said.

"Yes, you are," Granny replied.

Red awkwardly rejoined the group. "What does *liebling* mean?" she asked Sabrina.

"It's the German word for sweetheart," she explained.

Red's smile was so big, it looked as though it might split her face in two.

"Mr. Canis has something he'd like to say," Granny said, gesturing to the old man.

"Thank you, Relda. I know today is a day for mourning, but there are pressing matters that must be considered, the first of which is the identity of the Master. As you know, Red and I both suffer memory loss from the time we were ill. Red has come to me in hopes of restoring some of those memories. I believe, with the proper meditation techniques, she may be able to access some of her experiences. It was incredibly brave of her to approach me, considering our history together."

Sabrina studied the little girl. Red was a nervous wreck, but she was putting her fears aside to help. Sabrina wondered: Would she herself have the courage to trust a man who terrified her? She couldn't be sure.

"We will let you know if she uncovers anything useful," he continued. "I also have some troubling news to share. Our friends Mr. Boarman and Mr. Swineheart have come to me with fears that there have been some acts of sabotage within the camp."

"Sabotage?!" Henry said.

"What does *sabotage* mean?" Daphne asked.

"It's when someone intentionally tries to ruin a plan or destroy something important," Sabrina explained.

"Are you sure, old friend?" Granny said.

Canis nodded. "Several important parts of the main gate were stolen. The roof of the medical tent was tampered with, and there was some sort of effort to destroy the well with an explosive. The pigs assure me these are not mere accidents or poor workmanship. Someone is intentionally trying to make things difficult."

"Any suspects?" Veronica asked.

Everyone turned their eyes to Puck, who was making disgusting faces into Harry's mirror. He looked at them and grinned. "Thanks for the compliment, but it isn't me."

"I've looked at the damage myself," Canis said. "If I still possessed the Wolf's abilities, I might be able to pick up a scent from the saboteur, but I am just a man. It could be anyone, and with the steady influx of refugees, it's impossible to know for certain."

"You think one of the refugees is really working for this Scarlet Hand group?" Henry asked.

Canis nodded. "I ask you all to please keep this to yourselves. Charming, the pigs, Mr. Seven, and myself are the only ones who know, and we'd like to keep it that way. Knowledge of a spy in the community might create panic."

"Of course," Veronica said. "You can trust us with this secret."

Canis looked to Granny. "Lastly, Relda, I am afraid that, with this latest tragedy, I really need an answer to my question."

"What question?" Henry asked, suspiciously.

"As you know, the Everafters plan to confront the Master and the Scarlet Hand. It appears that peace is not a possibility. Our role in this community has always been to get involved when we feel we can be helpful," Mr. Canis said.

"What's that got to do with anything?" Henry asked.

"They want us to join their army?" Veronica guessed.

"No," Mr. Canis said. "As much as we need recruits, you're human, and far too fragile for this fight."

"Then what do you want us to do?" Daphne asked.

"We could lend Charming and his army some of the contents of the Hall of Wonders," Granny explained.

Henry nearly exploded. "That's nuts! Prince Charming is our family's bitterest enemy!"

"The prince is not the man you remember," Mr. Canis said.

"Am I really hearing you say this? You and Charming—best buddies?" Henry scoffed.

"He has earned my respect and my trust. He is not being deceitful when he says the Scarlet Hand is on the march. They won't be stopped until this town is in ashes, and I cannot sit idly by and let that happen. We come to your family because we are outnumbered. The Hand counts among its numbers the most ferocious of Everafters, the most powerful, and the most bloodthirsty. We need access to the Hall of Wonders to balance the scales. If we can't, there is little chance of defending Ferryport Landing."

"They only want a few items from select rooms," Granny explained to her family.

"Give it to them," Uncle Jake said.

Henry turned to his brother. "You agree with this?"

"Yes. Give it to them," Jake said. "Whatever they want. Anything to stop the Hand."

"I can't believe this!" Henry cried.

"We've taken the liberty of making a list," Mr. Canis said, holding out a sheet of paper.

Sabrina's father snatched it from his hands. "Thirty trained unicorns!"

"We have unicorns?" Daphne asked, amazed. "No one told me we had unicorns. Everyone knows I'm seven years old, right? Unicorns are everything to me."

Henry ignored her. "Two dozen Pegasus horses, the shoes of swiftness, Excalibur, the Wicked Witch's broom, Aladdin's flying carpet."

"Plus as many wands and enchanted weapons as you can spare," Mr. Canis said. "I'd also like the horn of the North Wind."

"Mom, you can't really be considering this!" Henry cried. "The only reason this town hasn't already destroyed itself is because everything is locked up in the hall. Who's to say that, once we turn this over to him, Charming won't use it to kill us all?"

"I'm to say," Mr. Canis said, tapping his cane on the floor angrily. "Do you believe I would allow harm to come to your family? Have I not proven myself to you a thousand times, Henry Grimm?"

"I don't think he's questioning your devotion, old friend," Granny said to Canis. "Henry is just voicing his fears. Giving over the keys, even to people we trust, is an enormous risk. It's also a departure from our family's traditional role. Which is why I have gathered you all here. We're going to vote on the request," Granny Relda announced. "I believe Jacob has cast his vote, so I turn to Daphne."

Daphne held her hand out to her grandmother. Granny seemed to understand what she wanted and reached into her handbag. She removed a small velvet bag and handed it to the little girl. Daphne opened it and took out a small silver kazoo. It looked like a toy, but Sabrina knew it was really the horn of the North Wind—a dangerous weapon. The Big Bad Wolf had used it to huff and puff his way into mayhem. Sabrina herself had accidentally destroyed a bank with one simple note. She wished that the army hadn't asked for it—this was the most powerful magical item she knew of, and it would be a catastrophe if the weapon fell into the wrong hands. Daphne, however, handed it to Canis, who thanked the little girl and tucked it into his suit jacket.

"You have my vote," she said.

Granny turned to Red. "And you?"

Red seemed overwhelmed to have been included. A happy tear streaked down her face. She nodded, another vote for the cause.

"Puck?"

The fairy boy shrugged. "Sounds fine to me, though if I had known that I could get at that stuff just by asking, I would have done it a long time ago."

Granny moved along. "Which brings us to Veronica."

Veronica looked at Henry, then back to the rest of the group. "The Master kidnapped Henry and me. He stole two years of my life and separated me from my daughters. I vote yes. Open every door, Relda."

Granny nodded. "Sabrina?"

Sabrina wanted to say no. She had seen what magic could do—the kind of chaos magic could incite. She herself struggled with an addiction to magic. But, what Canis was asking felt right, especially now that she had seen the destruction of Ferryport Landing.

"Sabrina, what do you say?" Henry asked.

"Give them the keys," Sabrina said.

Daphne looked at Sabrina as if she had never seen her before. It wasn't total forgiveness, but it wasn't the angry glare she'd been sporting for days.

Henry didn't have the same reaction. He scowled, clearly feeling betrayed by Sabrina's vote. When Relda turned to him, he voiced his dissent. "Dad would never approve of this. Releasing magic into this town is why he's dead."

Uncle Jake got up and left the cabin. Sabrina couldn't believe her father had thrown Basil's death into Uncle Jake's face, especially after Briar had died.

"But, I guess it doesn't matter what my vote is," Henry said. "I'm way outnumbered."

"Hank, your concerns are noted," Canis said. "Your involvement in our training would help to ensure your fears never come true. You could—"

"This is not my war, Canis," Henry interrupted.

"Then it's decided," Granny said. "Mr. Canis, tell Charming we'll give him what's on that list. I hope it helps."

"I pray it does," Canis said.

☙

"Did you say 'army'?" Mirror asked as he studied the list.

Granny nodded. A team of thirty or so soldiers along with Veronica, Sabrina, and Daphne stood behind her. The soldiers were a mixed lot—mostly Arthurian knights and Merry Men. Morgan le Fay was there, as well as Puss in Boots and the Scarecrow. There were a few fairies that Sabrina had never met, each more obnoxious than the last, and a rather smelly banshee. All of the visitors were completely bewildered when they stepped through the mirror into the Hotel of Wonders, and even more surprised when they went through another to enter the Hall of Wonders. Even Charming, whose own magic mirror was nothing short of incredible, was struck speechless.

"I had no idea," Mr. Seven said, marveling at the enormous hall.

"I never really get used to this place," Snow said, though she had once owned the mirror herself.

"I'm shocked. Bunny described this mirror as a botched first attempt," Charming said.

"A botched first attempt?" Mirror cried.

Charming ignored him. "But I think it will serve our needs very well. We could house an army ten times our size here, plus the weapons. It might be wise to train in here, too. There's plenty of space. OK, everyone, let's get to work."

"Relda, am I missing something?" Mirror asked.

Granny handed Mirror her massive key ring. "My family has agreed to aid Prince Charming's army with supplies and training. The list will tell you what they need."

Mirror looked skeptical. "No Grimm has ever gotten directly involved in the Everafter community in this manner. You can't just let this . . . this riffraff traipse in and out of here, taking whatever they like."

"No one cares about your opinion," Charming said, stepping up to Mirror. "You are a servant. Hurry along and get those doors opened."

"Billy Charming, you're forgetting your manners!" Granny cried.

"He's not a servant. He's our friend," Daphne said. "Be nice."

"Child, this so-called friend of yours is not real. He's nothing more than a security system designed to look after this hall and to obey your every command. He only has a personality to make dealing with him a bit more pleasant. His stubbornness, however, is obviously a malfunction, one we should have Bunny take a look at right away. He's wasting valuable time. My troops need to train."

Snow White stepped between the two men. "Billy, Mirror is a big part of this family, and he is well respected. Plus, I can attest firsthand that he's a sweetheart." She turned to face Mirror.

"Friend, we need your help. We're terribly outnumbered, and these rooms have the magical firepower to help us put up a good fight against the Scarlet Hand. I personally promise that everything will be returned in perfect condition."

"But—"

"Not even a scratch, Mirror," she said.

Mirror looked down at the keys and the list. He glanced at Granny Relda one last time, as if hoping she would come to her senses, but she just smiled.

"We really are in a bit of a rush," Granny said.

Mirror shrugged and shuffled off to do as he was told.

"Stop being mean to him," Daphne snapped at the prince.

Charming rolled his eyes.

Veronica stepped forward. "What can we do?"

Robin Hood smiled. "Your family is essential to our success. Few members of our army have experience with enchanted objects. You're going to train us, or I fear we'll all turn each other into frogs."

"We'll be happy to help," Granny Relda said.

The family spent the entire day instructing the Everafters in the proper use of magical gizmos. Sabrina did her best to help without actually touching anything, and so she eventually found herself giving people flying carpet lessons. Its magic never seemed to arouse her addiction, so she tried her best to teach steering, landing, and acceleration. She was terrible at it; nevertheless, the refugees treated her like a hero. They asked her millions of questions about her experiences. Everyone claimed to have heard one story or another about the sisters and were stunned to find out that most of them were true.

"Did you really kill a giant?"

"What did the Jabberwocky sound like?"

"Did Oz really build killer robots?"

Being the star should have been fun, but Sabrina couldn't help feeling like she was betraying her father with every new soldier she helped. Henry wouldn't even join them in the hall. Veronica guessed he was still in the courtyard, sulking. Sabrina thought of all the times she had done the same rather than lend a hand, and for the first time she understood how annoying it could be. She was tempted to go give her dad a lecture about having a good attitude. She could recite by heart many of the ones Granny Relda had given her, but she doubted it would do any good. They never really worked on Sabrina, either.

While Sabrina flew around the hall on the carpet, Daphne became the go-to expert on many of the other gizmos. The little girl's knack with wands and rings made her very popular with the recruits. Sabrina couldn't help but watch her with a mix of pride and regret for having treated her like a baby for so long. It was clear Daphne was growing up.

Granny Relda trained a band of Merry Men in the art of flicking a fairy godmother wand. It didn't come naturally to the burly men, whose weapons of choice were heavy clubs or bows and arrows. A wand required a delicate hand, and there was a lot of shouting when they couldn't get it quite right. Little John got so frustrated that he punched a nearby marble pillar.

Uncle Jake had more experience with magic than all the Grimms combined, especially when it came to enchanted creatures. He saddled unicorns and did his best to calm the nervous beasts. They were stubborn, dangerous animals. Elvis was frantic around them and hid behind Veronica when one trotted too close to him. Despite the obvious physical and emotional pain he was in, Jake never took a break, nor did he speak to anyone.

It was a long day. Most of the soldiers were hopelessly inept, and a few were already showing signs of magical addiction. There were far too many Everafters to teach and not enough time for anyone to master the new weapons. By dinnertime, Sabrina had only managed to teach fifty to fly on the carpet. Granny told her there were at least another three hundred waiting in line outside the mirror. Tomorrow was going to be even more exhausting.

Snow approached. "Looks like it's my turn." She seemed nervous.

"It's really simple," Sabrina said, hoping to ease her fear. "You just tell it what to do, and it obeys."

"If it's so simple, then why does it look so awkward?"

"That's me, I think," Sabrina said. "I'm not very good, and I can't seem to get it to work as well as Daphne. Even Uncle Jake says she's the best, but she's busy teaching the Scarecrow how to use a genie's ring. If you want to wait for her, I won't be offended."

"I think I'll stick with you," Snow said, stepping onto the rug. "So, how do we get it into the air?"

Sabrina joined her. "You just ask. Carpet, up!" Suddenly, the rug rocketed into the air and came to a screeching halt a few inches from the ceiling. Sabrina cringed. "Sorry—like I said, I'm not the best driver."

"Perhaps it's easier if we sit?" Snow suggested, easing herself down. Sabrina did the same. "So if I want it to go down the hall?"

"Just ask."

"OK, carpet, let's move," Ms. White said. The rug sailed forward, dipping and bouncing along the way. Sabrina remembered the time she and her family flew to Mexico on vacation. The plane sailed through some clouds and shook unpleasantly in the turbulence. Sabrina almost lost her lunch.

"Thank you for staying here to help," Snow said. "I know how much you and your father would rather get out of town."

"It's causing a lot of fighting between my mom and dad."

"I've noticed."

"My parents are a little obnoxious, huh?"

Snow laughed. "Don't worry, they'll work it out. I knew them before you were born. One look, and you could see how much they adored one another. I've only seen one other couple who looked at each other the way they do."

"You and the prince?" Sabrina asked.

Snow blushed. "What if I want to fly in a circle? Do I just ask, again?"

"Yep! When you're cruising along like this, it will follow your directions, but when things get crazy—like if you're being at-tacked—it has a mind of its own. I guess you could say it wants to save its own butt just as much you want to save yours."

Snow explained a route she wanted to take, and the rug fol-lowed her every instruction.

"So if you're in love with the prince, why aren't you getting married?" Sabrina asked.

"It's complicated."

"I've got time," Sabrina said. "I have to train Ichabod Crane next, and he sweats a lot when he's nervous. I'd rather put him off as long as I can."

"Well, it all started about six hundred years ago," Ms. White said with a laugh. "You see, there was a time when I was—well, pretty naive."

"Huh?"

"I was an idiot. In my defense, they didn't educate women back in my day. There used to be a joke in my village—the reason they were called the 'Dark Ages' is because the women couldn't figure out how to light the candles. Jokes weren't really that funny back then, either." Snow laughed at her own bad joke. "Anyway, I coasted on my looks and didn't worry about my brain. I was royalty, after all.

"And then, well, my mom gave me the poisoned apple to put me to sleep. I guess I had some kind of epiphany while I was sleeping, because a little while after Billy kissed me and woke me up, I got mad."

"That makes sense," Sabrina offered.

"No, I mean, I was mad at her for sure. But I was mad at Billy, too. And the universe. And the way things were done." Snow counted off on her fingers. "This guy shows up, and I'm supposed to marry him?! Just because he broke some spell? I expected my parents to pick a husband for me, but having the magical world make the decision felt even more unfair. Why couldn't I decide who I wanted to love? But even that's not what really, truly bothered me. It was the realization that I couldn't take care of myself. While I was riding off into the sunset on the back of Billy's horse, I made a decision. I would never allow myself to be a victim again."

"So you learned martial arts and started the Bad Apples self-defense school to teach other women how to fight back," Sabrina said, brightly. "And now you're training an army. But what does that have to do with Billy's proposal?"

"I broke my own promise. I let myself be victimized again."

"Bluebeard." His name sent shivers through Sabrina. It was only days ago that the infamous murderer had cornered Snow. Luckily, Prince Charming had appeared in the nick of time to save her.

"When he grabbed me and pulled me into that alley, I literally forgot all of my training. I was helpless," Ms. White admitted, ashamed.

"You shouldn't give yourself a hard time about it," Sabrina said. "He gave everyone the heebie-jeebies."

"I'm not everyone. I pride myself on my smarts and my right hook, but they both failed me. So I'm right back where I was six hundred years ago, with Billy saving my butt and expecting us to run off and get married."

"You're one of the bravest people I know," Sabrina said as she showed Snow how to make the carpet do a loop-the-loop.

"I'm not so sure that's true, Sabrina," Snow said. "And until I know, I can't get married, even though I love Billy. I won't marry someone who has to take care of me. I have to prove that I can take care of myself, again."

"I have a feeling Charming will wait for you," Sabrina said with a smile.

Snow smiled back.

All in all, the three heads of the army—Mr. Canis, Prince Charming, and Robin Hood—seemed happy with the day's progress. At the end of the very long day, the troops marched back through the portal to their well-earned cots. The Grimms were to sleep in the Hall of Wonders. Henry and Mr. Canis brought sleeping bags from the camp for each of them.

Mr. Canis informed the family that the mysterious saboteur struck several times that day but had yet to be identified. "Luckily," he said, "the destruction was repaired before anyone got hurt." Then Canis excused himself, as he and Red had work of their own to do.

Sabrina nestled into a sleeping bag next to her sister. Elvis lay between them, his big head resting on Daphne's belly.

"Daphne?" Sabrina called.

The little girl opened a single eye.

"Are you OK?" she said. "I mean, about Briar and—"

"No," the girl whispered. "It's very sad."

"You can talk to me if you want," Sabrina offered.

Daphne shook her head and rolled over so her back faced Sabrina. She wasn't ready to let go of her anger yet.

Feeling defeated, Sabrina turned her attention to the ceiling high above them. She was exhausted but too restless to sleep. Briar's funeral was still fresh in her memory. She thought about the princess, how she had foolishly sprung up to fight, even in the face of certain death. She hadn't given it a second thought, and now she was dead. Daphne, Snow, even Granny Relda were just like her, and Sabrina worried that one day their luck would run out as well. She desperately wanted to protect Daphne. It hurt that the little girl didn't understand. Yes, she wanted to go back to New York City to get away from all this madness, but it was also so Daphne would be safe—safe from the mobs of lunatics waiting outside their house, from the mayor who was trying to kill her. Daphne didn't get it. She thought Sabrina was being selfish and a coward. And maybe she was right.

Can I be a hero, too? Sabrina wondered. She knew she had done heroic things, but did she do them for others or to save her own behind? She suddenly understood that Daphne's cold shoulder was about more than stealing the horn of the North Wind from her, or siding with Dad to leave town. It was about right and wrong, about always doing the good thing even if it wasn't the wisest. Being heroic came so easily to Daphne. The gray areas didn't cause her to stumble the way they did Sabrina. Maybe the little girl was naive, but Sabrina suddenly understood that she might lose her relationship with Daphne if she didn't find the hero inside of her, and fast.

Someone rustled in a sleeping bag nearby. Sabrina turned and saw her mother stand up, slip on a pair of flip-flops, and pull a sweatshirt over her head. Sabrina's father was sleeping deeply beside her, and Veronica was trying to be quiet. She tiptoed down the hallway toward the Room of Reflections. Curiosity piqued, Sabrina shook her sister awake.

"Iiiiiiidooooghwannnagiiiiiiitupppfffff," Daphne grumbled.

"Wake up," Sabrina said.

"Didn't I tell you I'm mad at you?" Daphne muttered.

"Mom just snuck out of here. Let's follow her," Sabrina said.

"Maybe she's just getting a drink of water," the little girl complained.

"She's not after a glass of water. I know sneaking when I see it," Sabrina said, pulling Daphne out of her sleeping bag. "C'mon!"

Daphne grumbled but followed Sabrina down the hall to the Room of Reflections. They passed without disturbance into the Hotel of Wonders. Harry was nowhere to be found, so they hurried quickly through the portal that led to the fort. Outside, the night was chilly and damp.

"It's cold," Daphne complained. "Let's go back."

"Stop complaining. There she is," Sabrina said, following Veronica toward the medical tent. "Why is she going to see Nurse Sprat?"

"Maybe she's looking for another blanket," Daphne grumbled.

Sabrina grabbed her sister's hand and dragged her to the side of the tent. They got on their hands and knees and tucked their heads underneath a loose section of the canvas. Staying very still, they watched Nurse Sprat take their mother's blood pressure.

"Thanks for meeting me so late," Veronica said.

"Not a problem," the nurse replied. "But I do think this is something you should discuss with Henry."

"I will, but not until I'm sure."

The nurse nodded. "Have you been feeling funny since you woke up?"

"No, not at all," Veronica said, "which is what worries me. I should feel run down and nauseated, but I feel totally fine."

Daphne whispered, "What are they talking about?"

Sabrina shrugged and strained to hear more from the nurse.

"Well, I have to admit, this is the most unusual case I've seen. I don't think I know of anyone else who's ever been placed under a sleeping spell who happened to be pregnant at the time."

"Pregnant?!" the girls cried, then clapped their hands over each other's mouths. But it was too late. Veronica stood over them, hands on hips, disapproval all over her face.

7

VERONICA PULLED THEM INTO THE TENT. "What on earth do the two of you think you're do-ing?" she cried.

"You're going to have a baby?" Sabrina asked.

"I'm going to be a big sister, finally!" Daphne crowed.

"Girls, calm down," Veronica said.

"She's right, girls," Nurse Sprat said. "The miracle of life is the most unpredictable magic there is. We don't want you to get your hopes up too early."

"You were pregnant before you were kidnapped?" Sabrina asked.

Veronica nodded and finally surrendered to her daughters' curiosity. "I found out the day we were taken. I was so excited and knew Henry would be, too. I told him to meet me in Central Park after work so I could tell him the good news. We went to the carousel. It was a beautiful day. The last thing I remember is my friend Oz rushing down the hill toward us, and then we woke up here, in Ferryport Landing. And two years were gone."

Daphne and Sabrina shared an uncomfortable look.

"Oz is not your friend, Mom," Daphne said.

"He's the one who put you to sleep. He was working with the Master," Sabrina explained.

Veronica bit her lip and looked as if she might cry. "I trusted him," she whispered.

"So did we," Daphne said. "And then he attacked us with a giant robot. He's kind of a jerk."

"Mom, you've been asleep for almost two years. Do you think something's wrong with the baby?" Sabrina asked.

"I don't know," Veronica said. "That's what I'm here trying to figure out."

"I don't have a lot of experience with sleeping spells, but I suspect it's not the best situation to be in when trying to grow a baby," Nurse Sprat said. "The baby may have slept soundly, just like you and your husband. Most of the victims of these spells report that they didn't age a single day while they slept. Briar Rose, God rest her soul, was asleep for a hundred years, and she was just as young when she woke up as when she fell asleep. But she was an Everafter. We'll take a few tests, and we'll know more soon."

Veronica nodded. "But, girls, this has to be our secret, OK?

Your father is already beyond stressed, and he's dead set on escaping this town. I don't need him to snap and drag us through the woods again."

"I won't say a word," Sabrina promised.

"You can trust us," Daphne added, pretending to lock her lips with an imaginary key she then tossed behind her shoulder.

"How can we find out if the baby is OK?" Sabrina asked.

"Well, unfortunately, I don't have all the fancy machines I had at the hospital, but I did manage to grab some essential supplies before the Hand ran me out. I have a simple test that will tell us for sure. All I need is a blood sample."

Sabrina's mother rolled up her sleeve as Nurse Sprat prepared a needle. She took one small vial of crimson blood from the vein in the crease of Veronica's elbow, then bandaged the small wound.

"Give me three days," the nurse said, as she carefully labeled the vial with Veronica's name. "In the meantime, take it easy. Get some rest and stay off your feet. And let me know if you get a craving for pickles and ice cream."

"Thank you so much," Veronica said.

The girls followed their mother back out into the cool air. Sabrina had a million excited questions, and Daphne was skipping across the courtyard, but Veronica was quiet.

"Girls, come here," Veronica said, pulling her daughters close to her. The three Grimms hugged tightly.

"It's going to be all right," Daphne said, reassuringly. "I just know it."

"I hope you're right," Veronica said.

Sabrina hugged her mother with all her might. Even if the news about the baby was bittersweet and worrisome, they were together.

"Mom, look," Daphne said.

Sabrina turned to see where her sister was pointing. Across the courtyard was Briar Rose's fresh grave. Uncle Jake was sleeping on the ground beside it, with a rose resting on his chest.

Veronica frowned and led the girls back into Charming's cabin. It was empty except for the magic mirrors.

"I'm worried about him," Sabrina said.

"I'll tell your father," Veronica promised.

They slipped into the mirror that led to the Hotel of Wonders and found their way to the Room of Reflections. Mirror was there, busy with his work gluing shards to the walls.

"A little night air?" he asked. He smiled, as if he knew there was something more to the story.

Sabrina nodded. "We'll tell you soon."

He nodded and returned to his work.

They left the room, only to find Red Riding Hood rushing toward them. Mr. Canis hobbled along behind her. The little girl was sobbing uncontrollably.

"What's wrong?" Veronica said, swooping the girl into her arms.

"We've had a breakthrough," Mr. Canis said.

"He's everywhere," Red cried. "He can see everything."

"Who are you talking about?" Daphne asked.

"The Master. I remembered him!"

"You know who he is?" Sabrina asked hopefully.

"No! Just his eyes! I only saw his eyes. They were everywhere I went, watching me."

Red buried her face in Veronica's shirt and sobbed.

Veronica led the girls back through the Hall of Wonders to where the rest of their family lay asleep. She tucked her daughters back into their sleeping bags and kissed them good night. Then, she did the same for Red.

Wrapped in her sleeping bag, Sabrina dreamed of naked babies flying in and out of clouds. Their rosy cheeks beamed, and the sky was filled with giggles that transformed into tiny hearts and flowers. Sabrina had never cared much for babies—they were smelly and always covered in food. But the idea of having another little brother or sister was exciting. It was a wonder she could sleep at all.

Unfortunately, her lovely dreams were interrupted by a loud huffing sound and the sudden sensation of something moist and slippery rubbing against her cheek. Without opening her eyes, Sabrina grumbled, "Elvis, I'm sleeping. Go get Daphne to feed you." She pulled her sleeping bag up over her head. For a moment, she was sure the big dog was going to let her drift back to sleep.

But then, with a sudden jerk, her pillow was yanked out from under her head, and her skull rattled against the cold marble floor. Pain rocketed across her head. Furious, Sabrina sat up spewing threats of trips to the pound, when she realized that the culprit was not the Great Dane but an enormous white stallion hovering above her. It was held aloft by two powerful wings, and Sabrina recognized it as a Pegasus. Behind it hovered a dozen more, but only the one chewing on her pillow had a rider. Puck was sitting on its back, looking as if he was about to open his biggest Christmas present.

"What's the big idea?" Sabrina demanded. "Is this one of your stupid pranks?"

"I declared war on you, remember?" Puck said. "You contaminated me with your puberty virus, and you called my villainy into question."

"First of all, puberty isn't a virus," Sabrina said as she played tug-of-war with the Pegasus for her now rather damp pillow. "Second of all, I'm sorry if I gave the itty-bitty baby the boo-boo face."

Puck curled his lip in anger.

"Oh, now the baby is cranky," Sabrina taunted. "Perhaps we should put him down for a nap?"

"We'll see who's laughing soon enough," Puck said. "You see these flying horses?"

"Duh!"

"They have a very special diet. For the last two days, they have eaten nothing but chili dogs and prune juice."

Sabrina heard a rumble coming from the horse. It was so loud, it drowned out the sound of its beating wings. It whined a bit, and its eyes bulged nervously.

Puck continued. "Now, chili dogs and prune juice are a nasty combination. They can keep a human being on the toilet for a week. Imagine what would happen if I fed chili dogs and prune juice to a five-hundred-and-fifty-pound flying horse. Oh, wait a minute! You don't have to imagine it."

Puck's Pegasus let out a tremendous fart and then whined again.

The horror of Puck's plan sank in, and Sabrina panicked. She looked up at the fleet of horses and wondered if there was something she could do to save herself, but she couldn't think of anything. She heard a splat on the floor several yards away and quickly averted her eyes, but there was no escaping the smell. She feared it might never go away.

A second splat followed, and Sabrina scampered to her feet. The only strategy, she realized, was to stay mobile. She leaped out of the way just before a third horrible brown bomb crashed near her foot. But she found herself directly below another Pegasus about to blow. She rolled out of the way and collided with her sister.

"Geez, Sabrina. You should go see Nurse Sprat," Daphne said, pinching her nose.

"That's not me!" she cried. "We're under attack! Get up and save yourself."

Daphne gaped, unsure of what was happening, but when her sleeping bag suffered a direct hit, she dove to safety. In her efforts to escape the next attack, she knocked Sabrina down, and the two flailed like a couple of desperate fish in the bottom of a boat.

"There's nowhere to run," Puck shouted to the girls. "And, I'm not taking any prisoners." He laughed so hard, it echoed off the ceiling of the Hall of Wonders.

Another bomb fell with a disgusting splat.

"Is it on me?" Daphne cried, flipping her head back and forth. She calmed down when Sabrina assured her she had not been caught in the spray.

The commotion finally roused Granny Relda. "Puck! You cut this nonsense out at once!" she demanded, her shouts waking Henry and Veronica.

"Forget it, old lady. I'm done doing what I'm told," he shouted, steering his horse so that it flew uncomfortably close to the old woman. A splat landed mere inches from her feet, and she gasped in horror. She turned to Sabrina and gave her an impatient look.

"What did you say to him?" she asked.

Sabrina was shocked. "Why is it always me?"

"Because you're the only one who can get under his skin," Granny said. "You've obviously hurt his feelings. He's very sensitive."

"Sensitive? This kid hasn't brushed his teeth since the Civil War, and suddenly he cares about my opinion?" Sabrina asked.

"Why does he care so much what Sabrina thinks?" Henry asked, suspiciously.

Sabrina blushed and looked to the floor.

"You've got your first boyfriend!" Veronica exclaimed, clapping her hands happily.

"Ugh!" Henry complained. "I'm so not ready for this. Couldn't you have at least picked a boy who smells a little better?"

"I didn't pick anyone, Dad. I don't like him!" she cried.

Daphne grinned. "Whatever."

"Sabrina, apologize to him before this gets out of hand," Granny begged.

"Mom, this is already out of hand," Henry said, shielding himself and his wife with a sleeping bag. He shook a commanding finger at Puck. "Now, you listen to me, boy. This is unacceptable. You come down here and start acting your age!"

"Honey, he's over four thousand years old," Veronica said, cowering under the sleeping bag.

"Well, then, this is even more immature," Henry said.

Puck sailed over Sabrina's head. "I should thank you. You actually did me a favor."

"Oh, yeah?" Sabrina said suspiciously.

"I'd gotten too comfortable living in the old lady's house, eating the old lady's food, acting like a human. I am the Trickster King. The Crown Prince of Snips and Snails and Puppy-Dog Tails, the ruler of Gremlins, Rascals, and Miscreants, the guiding light of every instigator, agitator, and knave from here to Wonderland. I shouldn't be living with a bunch of heroes like you and your family. I should be causing the chaos you are trying to prevent. I am, after all, a first-rate villain."

"Fine, go be a villain!" Sabrina shouted. "But don't you think this is all a little overdramatic? Flying horses? Poop bombs?"

"Actually, I think it's just dramatic enough," Puck said. "Charge!"

There was little the Grimms could do. They ran around the Hall of Wonders in circles, shrieking. Eventually Mirror appeared, and despite his desperate cries and a very impressive bribe, the boy and his chili-dog-eating horses would not relent. Puck chased Sabrina until she tumbled over her own feet and fell. Helpless, she lay on the floor as the Pegasi drifted directly above her.

"Would saying I'm sorry make a difference?" Sabrina asked.

Puck cackled.

Like a lot of people who have lived through nightmarish things, Sabrina's brain mercifully blocked what happened next from her memory. She wouldn't remember being carried across the fort, where soldiers tossed bucket after bucket of soapy water on her until she was finally clean. She wouldn't remember how her family wrapped her in towels and carried her to a cot, where an elf sprayed her with several cans of air freshener. She wouldn't remember how her mother sang to her and fed her soup or that she slept for nearly twenty-three hours after the ordeal. It was good that she didn't remember, but those who witnessed it would be haunted by it for the rest of their lives. Daphne said she would never look at ponies—or chili dogs, for that matter—the same way again.

Sabrina *did* remember, however, her first glimpse of the saboteur. Once she had been hit, Sabrina had fled into the Room of Reflections, through the Hotel of Wonders, and out into the courtyard. Her family and friends followed, chased by Puck and his pooping Pegasi. Sabrina was racing toward the mess tent for cover when there was a terrible explosion from across the fortress. The newly built water tower suddenly caught fire and toppled over. It slammed into the ground and cracked open like a coconut, spilling hundreds of gallons of water into the courtyard. Everyone there was swept away by the flood and dragged nearly to the other end of the camp before they regained control of themselves. Sabrina scampered to her feet to help others when she saw a shadow dart away from the water tower. She couldn't see who it was, but she saw where he went. Daphne saw, too.

"I'll be right back," Daphne said, racing after the saboteur.

"Daphne, no!" Sabrina cried, but the little girl ignored her. She rushed after her sister. Daphne was fast, and Sabrina strained to keep up. She eventually lost her in the maze of equipment at the obstacle course, but when she heard Daphne shouting, she turned toward the noise and ran. She found her sister standing before the high fort wall with her hands on her hips.

"Where is he?" Sabrina asked.

"He either went over the wall"—Daphne pointed at the top, fifteen feet overhead—"or through that hole."

Sabrina spotted a small opening at the base of the wall where a portion of the timber had rotted. No normal-size person could have crawled through it—at least, not a human person. It was too small for even a child. Sabrina scowled. Whether the villain flew out or had the ability to shrink himself, it didn't matter. He was gone.

Charming appeared to supervise the cleanup. A small handful of Everafters came out of their tents to investigate, but he lied to them.

"Just a design flaw, people. Let's get it cleaned up," he told the gathering crowd, but when they drifted away, he turned to the girls. "You saw something, didn't you?"

"He was small and fast," Daphne said. "He got away."

Charming frowned and walked away.

Daphne looked down at herself. She was soaked from head to toe. "On the bright side, now we both need a bath."

❧

Days passed, and in that time, the refugees became near-experts on many of the magical items, including the flying carpet. Morgan le Fay worked closely with Mr. Seven, and soon the two of them could mount the unicorns with little trouble. Mr. Boarman and Mr. Swineheart kept busy designing and rebuilding a new water tower. They made various upgrades to the camp, including a deep moat around the perimeter, a new and bigger medical tent, and two more massive catapults, each loaded with boulders as big as a car. But the two little pigs were most proud of the high-pressure water cannons they attached to the watchtowers. They would help fend off dragons if any happened to attack.

The biggest change, however, was in the mood of the recruits. Gone were the frightened refugees eager to avoid confrontation. Briar's death and all their training had transformed them into a determined bunch. They were itching for a fight with the Scarlet Hand. With each passing hour, they became a real army, and the camp became an imposing fortress.

Sabrina should have been proud of the community, but as things changed around her, they became eerily familiar. The fortress she and Daphne had visited in Ferryport Landing's dark future seemed to spring up around her. Some things were different. For example, Snow White was still alive, and Granny Relda wasn't planning missions, but there were moments when Sabrina was sure she had stepped through a hole in time again. She worried that Charming, Daphne, and her own efforts to change the future were not enough to avoid their disastrous destiny.

The family sat down in the mess tent for a breakfast of oatmeal and wild berries, eggs, and juice. Everyone she cared about was there, even Uncle Jake, though he just picked at his food listlessly. The only person missing was Puck, which was fine by Sabrina. He swore his war with her was not over. She counted her lucky stars that he wasn't hovering over her, preparing to ruin her meal with some disgusting prank. Relieved, she scooped up a big spoonful of oatmeal, but after that first bite, she felt something pop inside her mouth. She didn't think much of it, until she noticed her mother staring at her in shock.

"What?"

"Oh, my," her father said. "Mom, what's in this oatmeal?"

"It's just oatmeal," the old woman promised.

Sabrina looked at her hands. They were a shade of murky green. Uncle Jake took her hand in his own and flipped it over. "Puck."

It was all the explanation she needed. Sabrina leaped up from her seat and ran to Charming's cabin. She needed to see herself in one of the mirrors. When she did, she let out a shriek. Her face, hands, feet, and even her ears were swampy green. She looked like a frog.

Reggie's face appeared in his mirror. "Girl, you look like you were wrestling with a bunch of broccoli. You kids will jump on the latest fad no matter how silly you look."

"This isn't a fashion statement," Sabrina cried.

She heard Puck laughing at her from the door of the cabin, and she spun around to face him.

"What did you do to me?" she asked.

"Don't get all freaked out, Grimm. It'll wear off by the time you start college," Puck said.

The rest of the family pushed their way into the cabin.

"Looks like he slipped you a water toadie egg," Uncle Jake said.

Granny smiled weakly. "It's not harmful. We have a remedy in the hall, but—"

"But what?"

"Well, the remedy has side effects," Uncle Jake explained.

"What kind of side effects?"

"You'll grow a tail!" Puck smirked.

Sabrina was about to strangle Puck, but Prince Charming stormed into the cabin, demanding that someone do something about Goldilocks. "She's moving everything around!"

Goldie followed close behind. "This camp's energies are out of balance. You can't have the catapult near the water tower. Water has a calming effect on people. You should put the catapult somewhere where people are excited—like the fire pit."

"See? She's talking nonsense!"

"It's not nonsense! It's feng shui, and it's thousands of years old," Goldilocks said. "It can help everything and everyone stay in their harmonics."

"This is a military complex. It's not supposed to have harmonics."

"You asked me for my help, William," the woman said stubbornly.

"This isn't what I had in mind. I need fighters, especially ones with unique talents. You can command an animal army, but instead you're moving the ammunition and the horses so they are one with the universe. Woman, we're launching an attack tonight!"

"What!" Henry cried. "You didn't tell us that!"

"I'm not in the habit of discussing my plans with you," Charming snapped, then turned to Sabrina. He examined her from head to toe. "You are such a strange child."

Sabrina growled. Puck laughed again.

Charming turned his attention back to Henry. "Hood and the Merry Men only found one of the hobgoblins you let get away. The other has assuredly returned to the Hand to report where we are located. They are likely organizing to attack us as we speak, and I have no intention of sitting and waiting for it to happen. We're going to strike first. It may be our only opportunity to surprise them."

Granny gave Sabrina the antidote for her green skin. It was a thick, coppery-tasting concoction that changed her skin back to normal within a few seconds. The side effect, however, could appear at any time. Sabrina knew if she sat around worrying about when it would sprout, she would go crazy, so she plunged into training to keep herself distracted. It was a particularly busy day as everyone prepared for the battle ahead.

As the hours ticked by, Sabrina noticed an odd phenomenon coming over the refugees. The Everafters couldn't help being totally honest with one another. Perhaps, with so much on the line, they were giving their lives a second look. Everafters rushed around confessing their undying love for one another. Ms. White and Beauty were nearly mobbed with not-so-secret admirers. Even Mr. Seven mustered the courage to ask Morgan le Fay to take a walk with him around the camp. It seemed like an odd pairing, but the beautiful witch looked flattered when she accepted his invitation.

Still, some soldiers were panicked. Snow gathered them together for a pep talk. She didn't lie. She told them that the battle would be dangerous and that people might be injured, but everyone was well trained. She told them that fighting back was a tremendous risk but that they would be celebrated as heroes wherever Everafters lived, in Ferryport Landing and beyond. Sabrina watched their nervous faces harden and the fear in their eyes transform into fierce determination. When Snow walked away, the group was demanding to be launched at the Scarlet Hand. They couldn't wait to fight. Perhaps it was that Ms. White was a natural leader, or it was the effect of her many years as a teacher, but the refugees believed in her. It was hard to reconcile this woman with the one who not so long ago expressed her own fear and self-doubt to Sabrina.

"She's impressive," Charming said as he watched Snow rally the troops.

"You should tell her that yourself," Sabrina said.

"I don't want to encourage it. She could get hurt. I want to keep her safe."

"That's not what she needs from you," Sabrina said.

"You're just a child. What do you know?" Charming snapped. After a long moment he spoke again. "Did she say something to you?"

Sabrina nodded. "Yes, but I don't think she'd appreciate it if I repeated it to you. Let's just say that treating her like a china doll is not going to work."

"It feels like keeping her safe is in my blood, sometimes. It's not an easy thing to turn off," he admitted. "How do I protect a woman who doesn't want to be protected?"

Mr. Seven approached. "The army is moving into the Hall of Wonders as you asked," he reported.

"Very good, my friend," Charming said, patting Mr. Seven on the back. "I think tonight a few of us are going to become legends—including you. But, if you get killed out there, I'm going to fire you."

"I don't work for you anymore," Seven said, smiling.

"Details, details," Charming said, holding out his hand.

Seven nodded, and the two men shook respectfully, and then Mr. Seven raced away.

The troops gathered beneath the vaulted ceiling of the Hall of Wonders. Charming, Snow White, Robin Hood, and Mr. Canis stood at the front of the crowd.

The prince called for everyone's attention. "You have all worked hard to learn to fight. Now it's time to learn how to win."

Sabrina and her family watched from the back of the crowd. Mirror joined them and seemed quite interested in the plan. Charming explained it in complicated detail, but when he finished, Sabrina understood that the assault would be on the Ferryport Landing Marina. It sat on the very edge of town. Charming reported that spies had discovered that Everafters living outside of the town were secretly shipping supplies and magical weapons to the Hand. If the troops could destroy the dock, there would be no place for the supply ships to land, thus cutting off a valuable source of aid to the Master and his evil army.

To accomplish this, the army needed a four-pronged attack. The first battalion would be commanded by Goldilocks. She would use her unique ability to speak with animals to direct an air force of birds. They would distract the Hand's guards so that

Robin Hood could launch a second assault with his trained archers, raining arrows down on any Scarlet Hand soldiers guarding the marina. Next, Mr. Seven would lead a team of Lilliputians, mice, and other very small Everafters down to the docks, where they would attach explosives underneath the dock itself.

"Then, we drop the hammer," Prince Charming explained. "Arthur's knights will storm the docks, drawing out more of the Hand's forces. When the time is right, our troops will make a sudden retreat, just before the bombs explode."

"And what do I do?" Snow asked. She was visibly angry. "I'm not going to sit by while everyone else risks their lives."

"Relax, Ms. White," Charming said. "You've got the best job of the whole attack. You get to detonate the explosives."

"Oh." Snow smiled. "I'm a big fan of this plan."

"What about you, Canis?" Puss in Boots asked the old man. "What's your part in this plan?"

"My assistant and I will be fighting our own battle tonight," the old man replied, placing his hand on Red Riding Hood's shoulder. "Red has made tremendous progress. We hope that tonight we may be able to finally access her memories and reveal the identity of the Master."

Prince Charming gestured into the crowd. "And now, Friar Tuck will lead us in a prayer."

A bald, overweight man with a veiny nose stepped forward.

His kind eyes scanned the crowd. "Let us join hands and lower our heads."

Sabrina took Daphne's hand and Mr. Boarman's. Geppetto held hands with the Scarecrow. Rip Van Winkle held hands with Jack Pumpkinhead. Beauty held hands with Frau Pfefferkuchen-haus, and together they all prayed. Though they each held their own beliefs and traditions, they quietly asked for their own safety and the safety of the others, for the success of their fight, and for the enlightenment of their enemies. Sabrina did the same. She hadn't been to church since her parents' abduction and wondered if anyone in heaven would still listen to her, but she closed her eyes and whispered her hopes anyway.

When it was over, the troops donned their armor, picked up their shields and weapons, and marched through the portals and then on through the massive gates of the camp. Sabrina and her family stood by, waving to everyone and wishing them luck. So many familiar faces passed by, and there was no guarantee they would ever return.

Pinocchio watched as his father marched to war. Geppetto's uniform was too big, and he was having a difficult time with his bow and quiver, but he continued onward.

"Be a good boy," he said, hugging his son.

"Farewell, Papa!" Pinocchio replied.

"They're not ready," Sabrina whispered to her grandmother.

The old woman nodded sadly. "No one is ever ready for war."

Uncle Jake trailed behind the army. When Granny spotted him with the other soldiers, she began to cry.

"This is not your fight, Jake," Henry called out to him.

Uncle Jake turned and pointed at Briar's grave. "It is now."

Hours passed, and the family huddled together in the mess tent, waiting for word of the battle. They said nothing to one another, but their worried eyes spoke loud and clear. Even Elvis was fidgety, chomping at a fly that kept landing on his nose.

After some time, Pinocchio approached, and his smiling face dissolved some of the tension. Sabrina wondered how he could be so carefree with his father in so much danger.

"I come bearing gifts," the little boy said, setting his burlap sack on a table. "They're not much, but I hope you enjoy them."

He handed a marionette to Sabrina. She peered at it closely and smiled when she realized it looked just like her. The figure had blond hair and blue eyes and even had her dimple on its right cheek. She marveled at its intricacies all the way down to the dingy sneakers and her favorite blue shirt.

"I love it!" Daphne said, when Pinocchio handed her one that looked just like her.

Granny Relda smiled as she looked down at her marionette. It wore a bright pink dress with a matching hat—complete with a sunflower painted in its center.

"I wanted to thank you. You have all been such wonderful friends to my dear father," the boy said as he reached into his sack and took out marionettes for Henry and Veronica. Puck's featured his filthy green hoodie. There was even one for Elvis.

"It's nearly as good-looking as I am," Puck said, admiring his gift.

"Pinocchio, these are truly remarkable," Granny said.

"You must have worked so hard," Veronica added.

"One can be quite industrious with the right inspiration," the boy said.

"I don't know what to say," Henry said. He moved the strings, and his marionette did a funny little dance.

"If I knew we were giving presents, I would have gotten you something," Sabrina said, slightly embarrassed.

"Well, there is something you could do to return the favor," the boy said.

"Name it," Daphne said.

"I was hoping Sabrina might give me some instruction on flying the magic carpet. I'm quite curious about it but did not want to get in the way of the soldiers. Could I trouble you for a lesson?"

"Look at all these doors!" Pinocchio cried as he and Sabrina soared through the Hall of Wonders aboard the carpet. "How many do you think there are?"

"I don't know," Sabrina said. "My grandmother says there are hundreds, but even she isn't sure."

"What do you suppose is behind all of them?"

"Trouble, for the most part."

"It must be thrilling to have access at your leisure," the boy said. "I'm quite envious of the freedoms your family has granted you. I have been held back at nearly every turn in this life. It can be quite perplexing."

Sabrina laughed. "You've got one big vocabulary there, Pinocchio."

Pinocchio blushed. "I've picked up a few words here and there. Being so young in appearance has been nothing short of frustrating. Surely, you understand. Adults presume that since you look like a child, you have the interests of a child or, worse, need to be protected like one."

"Well, adults like to make rules, but I guess it's usually to keep kids safe," Sabrina said.

Pinocchio scowled. "Well, I am not exactly a child. I'm nearly two hundred and fifty years old! I have a passion for art and music, culture, and politics. Besides this stupid, childish form, I am an adult in every way!"

The rug seemed to sense his anger, and it dipped and flipped, crashing to the ground and sending the children skidding across the floor. Both Sabrina and Pinocchio were uninjured.

"The carpet likes its driver to be calm," Sabrina explained.

Pinocchio blushed again. "I apologize."

Sabrina shrugged. "I get plenty mad sometimes, too. Don't worry about it."

She crossed the hall to fetch the rug, which was wadded beneath one of the many doors. It was the one with two stones set into the wood, each with a hand carved into the surface. She had spotted it briefly when the family first arrived at this end of the hall, and she remembered that the plaque didn't say what was behind it. She studied the door closely, looking for some kind of clue to solve the mystery.

"That's odd," Sabrina said.

"What's odd?" Pinocchio said.

"There's no keyhole in this door," Sabrina said. "And there's nothing to tell me what's behind it."

"Yes, a gripping mystery," Pinocchio said, sarcastically.

"Yeah, sure," Sabrina said to the boy. He might not have understood how intriguing this door was, but she knew that the rooms often contained something dangerous. The plaques were essential to warning whoever opened those doors about what they might find.

"We should get back to the camp," Pinocchio said. "Thank you for the lesson."

At that moment, Daphne raced to join them. "Come quick! The army is back!"

One step into the real world and Sabrina's throat tightened from the smell of smoke. Pained cries filled her ears. She watched as dozens of Everafters were carried into the fort on stretchers.

"What happened?" she asked, but the soldiers were either too busy or too exhausted to explain. They rushed past, jostling her.

"Close the gates!" Charming shouted once everyone was inside. The guards quickly slammed the immense doors and braced them tightly with a bar as big as a tree. The prince commanded everyone to take positions around the fort wall in case the Hand had followed them.

"What happened, William?" Granny Relda asked.

Charming scowled. "They knew we were coming. They were ready, and they beat us, badly. I have no idea how many are wounded or dead."

"How could they know?" Daphne cried.

Uncle Jake appeared, his face full of disgust. "Nottingham and his thugs were on us the second we arrived. They countered our every move, as if they knew our whole strategy."

"Whoever's causing all the trouble inside the camp must be a spy, too," Sabrina said.

Nurse Sprat raced to the group. "I can't handle all of these people," she said. "There's only one of me."

"I'll help," Granny said. "I worked for the Red Cross during the war."

"You can count on all of us," Veronica added. "Just tell us what to do."

The rest of the day, Sabrina and her family ran for medicine, helped dress wounds, and did whatever they could to make the suffering Everafters comfortable. Twenty were critically wounded, and dozens more needed stitches or splints. One of Robin Hood's Merry Men was hurt badly. Little Boy Blue had two broken ribs. A few of the Everafters died while Nurse Sprat tried to save them, including Frau Pfefferkuchenhaus. The gingerbread witch had taken a blow to the head and fallen into the river. She was too far gone when she arrived back at the camp.

The nurse wept, cursing the Master and his Scarlet Hand. "I'm not a trained doctor," she cried. "I can only do so much." No one blamed her. They were grateful for what she could do, and by the end of the day, she had saved the lives of twenty-six people.

Exhausted, Sabrina and her family stumbled back to the Hall of Wonders. There they found a hundred and fifty or so soldiers, all of whom looked beaten down and afraid. Charming, Ms. White, Mr. Seven, and Mr. Canis looked over them like shepherds tending a flock.

"I hear that things did not go well," Mirror said when they arrived.

Uncle Jake nodded. "It's true."

"Charming wants to meet with you to discuss the next mission," Mirror replied.

"Next mission?" Henry exclaimed. "The last plan nearly got everyone killed."

"Then I suggest you use the time to talk some sense into the prince," Mirror said. "He can't send these people into battle again. They're not soldiers."

"Shut up, Mirror," Uncle Jake spat.

The little man was dumbfounded. "Jacob, I—"

"We are in the middle of a war, Mirror. If they hear you telling them it's hopeless, you are going to crush their spirits," Jake said, then stormed away.

Mirror shook his head but didn't say any more.

"I'm sorry, Mirror," Granny said to him. "My son is going through some very difficult things right now. I'm sure he didn't mean to be so rude."

Standing in front of his army, Charming raised his hand until he had everyone's attention. "Tomorrow we march on the sheriff's office."

The crowd gasped in unison.

"Are you crazy?" Puss in Boots shouted.

"That's suicide," Ichabod Crane yelled, nursing a wounded arm. "You saw what they did to us. We're no match for them!"

The Scarecrow stepped forward. "My calculations tell me we have a ten percent chance of surviving another confrontation with the Hand."

"I've been informed that the sheriff's office is the headquarters for the Hand," Charming announced. "If we can destroy it, we take a valuable asset away from them. If we can capture Nottingham as well, it would be a vicious blow to their strategy. Mr. Seven and I have considered several approaches and have devised a four-pronged attack."

"You and your four-pronged attacks!" Beauty cried bitterly. "William, please! Listen to reason!"

Charming continued. "The first attack comes from the Pied Piper, who will command rats and squirrels to infest the office, driving Nottingham and whoever else might be inside out into the open. Once they are in the street, the second attack comes from the sky. Buzzflower and Mallobarb will lead a squadron of flying wizards and witches over the crowd, zapping as many of the Hand as they can with their wands. The third attack will then commence with Goldilocks and the bears, along with an army of intelligent animals, attacking Nottingham directly. And finally, the fourth prong—Mr. Seven and Robin Hood will lead our knights, archers, and swordsmen into the fray."

"Are you determined to get us all killed?" Rip Van Winkle cried.

The prince's jaw stiffened, but Snow White stepped forward before he could respond. There was an angry fire burning in her eyes.

"You have two choices. Die under the heel of the Master or fight. That's it. There are no other alternatives," she shouted. "Make your choice right now. This is the plan. If you think you have a better chance on your own, then pack up and get out of this camp!"

The crowd grew quiet, but no one left.

"The camp is not safe tonight," Snow continued. "Pack your things. We're all moving here, into the Hall of Wonders. Do it quickly. You need your sleep. We march at dawn."

8

ENRY SHOOK HIS HEAD IN DISBELIEF. HE stormed away from the family and out through the portal. When he hadn't returned an hour later, Sabrina went looking for him. He wasn't at the camp or in the Hotel of Wonders, either. Soon, she found herself back in the Room of Reflections. There, she found Mirror removing a broken shard from the frame of one of the ruined mirrors.

"Why aren't you with your family, Sabrina?"

"I'm looking for my dad," Sabrina said. "He's pretty upset, and I'm worried about him."

"Yes, he's not a happy camper. I took him back to your grandmother's house some time ago. Come along, and I'll take you, too."

Mirror led her back into the hall and away from the crowds until they found the trolley. In no time, they were zipping down the hall.

"I'm sorry Uncle Jake snapped at you earlier," she said. "He's very . . ."

"He's upset, Sabrina, and he has every right to be. Just like you do. I haven't had a chance to say how sorry I am about Briar Rose. It's a terrible tragedy," Mirror said.

Sabrina nodded and tried not to cry.

"But he's not the only one suffering, is he?" Mirror continued. "I know you were hoping for a brighter reunion with your parents."

"You're reading my mind," Sabrina said.

"If I said your sister's cold shoulder was bothering you, too, would I qualify as a full-fledged psychic?"

Sabrina nodded. "You've been paying attention."

"I see everything that goes on around here," Mirror said. "Sabrina, do you believe in happy endings?"

"You mean like in fairy tales?"

Mirror nodded. "Quite a number of them have happy endings. Even the story they wrote about me has a happy ending for Snow and the prince."

"I don't think it worked out as well as in the story. The two of them are barely speaking."

"They'll work it out. Those two are meant for each other. I'm talking about you, Sabrina. Do you believe happiness is in your future?"

"I used to," Sabrina said. "I thought that when my parents woke up, things would go back to normal. We'd all move back to the city, and Granny and Uncle Jake would come for visits. That was my happy ending."

"And you've given up on it?" Mirror asked.

Sabrina shrugged.

Mirror sighed. "I believe everyone deserves a happily ever after. But I also believe that happy endings don't just happen by accident—you have to make them happen."

"I'm not sure what you mean," she said.

"Your happiness is your responsibility," Mirror explained as he brought the trolley to a stop. "If you want to be happy, you have to work to make it happen. You can't just wish for it, and you can't put it in the hands of other people. It took me a long time to realize that myself."

"You?"

"Sure, even a magic mirror has dreams," he said. "I'd hate to see you grow bitter waiting for yours to come true. If you want a happy ending, you have to work for it. Luckily, if Sabrina Grimm sets her mind to something, there's nothing that's going to get in her way."

Sabrina smiled. Mirror always made her feel better. She felt like she could tell him anything and he'd understand. In many ways, he was the closest thing she had to a best friend.

"So, I suppose you'd like me to wait while you talk to your dad?" Mirror asked.

"You're the best." Sabrina hugged the little man and climbed down from the trolley.

"Hurry up, the meter is running," he joked.

Sabrina hopped through the portal and into Granny Relda's spare bedroom. The power was still out, so everything was dark. The air was stuffy, too. From the shouting and explosions outside, it was clear that the Scarlet Hand was still trying to find a way inside, but the protective spells were working to keep them out.

Sabrina called for her father and listened for his reply. She followed his voice to her bedroom—rather, his bedroom. He was lying on the bed staring up at his model airplanes. A photo album rested on his chest. He turned his head when she entered and smiled.

"Need a friend?" Sabrina asked.

"I didn't think I had any friends left."

"I know that feeling," Sabrina said. She noticed the collection of marionettes Pinocchio had made of her family resting on the nightstand.

"I didn't want anything to happen to them," her father explained. "Pinocchio worked so hard."

Sabrina climbed onto the bed next to her father.

"I know you're worried about our family. I know you don't want me and Daphne to get involved with this war," she said. "But, Dad, you have to understand how confusing it is. You and

Mom encouraged us to be brave and kind and help other people. You taught us right from wrong. Granny and Mr. Canis have been teaching us the same things. Now, you're asking us to stop. I want to listen to you. I would love to go back home and forget about this place, but the thing is . . . I can't. Daphne's right. We're supposed to be here."

Her father rubbed his face in his hands, something he did when he was trying to wrap his head around a problem.

"You think I'm a coward," he said.

Sabrina was going to argue, but she wasn't sure he was wrong.

"It's not the fight that worries me, Sabrina," he said. "It's the magic."

He sat up and flipped through the photo album. Inside were yellowing photographs of the Grimm family from long before Sabrina was born. Her father stopped at a picture of himself and Jacob as kids, dressed in long wizard robes and pointy hats decorated with tinfoil stars and moons. Each boy held a magic wand in his hand and was pointing it playfully at the camera.

"I was around Daphne's age when my father opened the Hall of Wonders to your uncle and me. Back then, we only locked the doors that had dangerous weapons or creatures, so Jake and I ran wild in there. It was a giant playground, and we didn't have to share the slide with other kids. I learned to conjure fireballs and handle dragon eggs before I hit the third grade. Mom and Dad thought it was good for us to know how to use magic."

There was a picture of the two boys sitting atop a griffin. Despite its dangerous claws and vicious beak, Jake and Henry looked like they were riding a pony on a carousel. Their father, Basil, stood by proudly.

"What they didn't teach us was that we needed to take magic seriously. It was all a game to us," he continued. "There didn't seem to be any consequences. But there are consequences, Sabrina, deadly ones."

"Dad, I know what happened with Grandpa and Uncle Jake," she said. "It was an accident."

"But people are supposed to learn from accidents, Sabrina. We're not supposed to repeat our mistakes over and over again. Even after freeing the Jabberwocky and losing my father, this family got right back to fooling around with magic. And now, my own daughters are using it. That's why I want to get us out of this town. I want to leave before you have to pay the consequences, too."

"Would Grandpa Basil want us to leave?"

Henry was quiet. He flipped through the photo album and stopped on a picture of his father. Basil was standing in the front yard with an ax in his hand.

"Daphne and I take magic very seriously," Sabrina continued. "I learned the hard way. I can't go near most of the stuff, but Daphne . . . sure, she gets excited when she gets to use it, but it's not a game to her. She respects it, Dad. And she's really good with it. Even better than Uncle Jake."

"But what if things go wrong?"

"That's life. Things go wrong all the time. Sometimes you think something is going to be a certain way, and it turns out completely different. You have to just pick yourself up and keep trying. No one knows that better than me. That's why I voted to be part of this. If we don't teach the Everafters how to fight, they will lose. And we need them to win, Dad. The whole world needs them to win."

Henry stared at his daughter for a long moment. "When did you get so smart?"

Sabrina shrugged. "My dad's pretty bright. Plus, Mirror gives amazing advice."

Henry hugged her tight. It felt good. Maybe she'd get the reunion she'd wanted all along.

"OK, new rules," he said. "I'll get used to the fact that my daughters are tougher and smarter than I remember—"

"And older, too," Sabrina interrupted. "I know it's tough getting used to the fact that two years have passed, but you're driving Daphne nuts when you call her a baby. She's very sensitive about it."

"OK, I'll try, if you promise to still love me, no matter how obnoxious I am. Agreed?"

"Agreed," Sabrina said. "Oh, and stop arguing with Mom. It's getting boring."

Henry laughed. "Don't sugarcoat it, Sabrina. Tell me how you really feel."

"I'm just calling it as I see it. I'm sure I inherited that from Mom," she said.

"Do you have keys to any of the rooms with you?" Henry asked.

Sabrina took her huge key ring from her pocket. "Yeah, why?"

"There are a few other items this army could use," Henry said.

She followed her father back into the Hall of Wonders. He led her from room to room, collecting a variety of magical objects, some she had used before, but others she had never even seen.

One of them was a gizmo Henry claimed came from Oz. "It used to belong to H. M. Wogglebug, who used it to make himself bigger. He's a giant bug," he explained.

Then he led her to another room where he retrieved a small vial labeled THE POWDER OF LIFE. Henry claimed it could bring inanimate objects to life, like the Sawhorse and Jack Pumpkinhead. He hoped it might be used to create a few more soldiers for the army. The more rooms they visited, the more excited Henry grew, and Sabrina started to wonder if she really knew her father at all. Gone was the lovable-but-boring guy who always played by the rules. In his place was a determined fighter eager to do the right thing. Whoever this new dad was, she hoped he was here to stay.

"Wow, you really like your sleep," Uncle Jake said, holding his right cheek. He was standing over Sabrina in the dark.

"What time is it?" she asked, sitting up.

"Wake your sister. We have a mystery to solve."

After much vigorous shaking, Daphne was on her feet, and the sisters followed Uncle Jake into the camp. Sabrina expected to find it deserted this late in the night, but it was a flurry of activity. Everyone was rushing about with buckets of water, doing their best to put out a fire raging through the vegetable garden.

"The saboteur has struck again," Uncle Jake said.

"Fudge," Daphne complained. "This guy is really starting to get on my nerves."

"He freed the chickens from the henhouse, too. But that's not even the worst of it. Look!" Uncle Jake pointed to the ground just outside the armory—a shed that stored the soldiers' weapons. Piles of arrows lay broken on the ground. Sabrina knew at once that these had belonged to the Merry Men. They were a major part of the next day's attack, and now they were useless.

"Did you see anything?" Sabrina asked her uncle. She suspected he'd spent another night beside Briar's grave.

He shook his head. "I dozed off. The fire was already raging when I woke up. Whoever is sabotaging us has gotten away with it three times. We need to put the Grimm detective skills to work."

Daphne clapped her hands. "Yay!"

"I'll comb through the garden," Uncle Jake said. "Daphne, you take the henhouse, and, Sabrina, you search the armory. If you find any clues, whistle."

The trio sprang into action, and Sabrina rushed to the armory. She was surprised to find the large metal lock on the door completely intact. How did the saboteur get to the arrows without opening the door? Perhaps, she thought, they had a key. Charming, Seven, Robin Hood, Ms. White, and maybe a few others had keys, but none of them seemed the type to betray the refugees. Charming hadn't always been entirely trustworthy, but he had built this camp. He was too proud to sabotage it.

She circled the building, looking for another way in. She found a slightly ajar window on the far side and forced it all the way open. She clambered into the dark, dry room. There wasn't much light, and the moon, hidden behind clouds, was not helping. She tried to feel around, but without light her investigation was pointless. She decided to come back when the sun was up.

As she made her way back to the window, she stepped on something. It gave way, and she lost her footing, tumbling onto her backside. She quietly cursed in pain as she groped in the dark for whatever had tripped her. She found something small, sleek, and smooth—like wood. She shoved it into her pocket and crawled back to her feet. Soon, she was out the window and rushing to find her sister and uncle.

"I couldn't see a thing in the chicken house," Daphne said.

"And there was nothing near the garden," Uncle Jake said. "I'll have to wait until they put the fire out to search the rest of it."

"Well, that was a bust. You want to come into the hall and sleep with the rest of us?" she asked her uncle.

"Yeah, you're going to get the flu sleeping out here," Daphne scolded.

Uncle Jake shook his head. "No, I . . . I need to be near her."

He turned and walked back to Briar's grave.

Morning came faster than Sabrina expected. Henry and Daphne went to work training as many of the refugees as they could in the use of the new weapons Henry had supplied, but his newfound enthusiasm was not enough to raise morale. Charming's failed mission had them in a funk, and the cold rain and fog drifting into camp didn't help. It was a miserable day, and it was reflected on the faces of the already-reluctant army. The first battle was a disaster, and now, as they went off into a new fight, lingering feelings of humiliation and hopelessness weighed on their shoulders.

"I couldn't get them into a fighting mood," Ms. White said as she and the girls watched the army file out through the gates. "They need to feel they can win this fight, or they won't." She spotted Uncle Jake marching with the crowd and rushed to join him.

Soon, the heavy gates of the camp were closing. Aside from a handful of elderly guards deemed too feeble to fight and a small group of Everafter children—which included Red and Pinocchio—the Grimms were left alone once more to wait for news.

Granny spent most of the day studying a three-dimensional map of the town that Mr. Seven had constructed. She fretted over Charming's plan, imagining all the possibilities. When a new strategic idea came to her, she told one of the Everafter birds, who flew off to deliver her message to the prince.

Daphne, Puck, and Elvis played a game in which they tossed an old pie tin through the air to see who could catch it in their teeth first—the big dog or the fairy. Pinocchio was invited to join, but he refused, claiming he was not interested in baby games. Instead, he wandered from one adult to the next, eager for an intellectual conversation about art or science or chess. He found no takers. Sabrina felt a pang of sympathy for him. She knew what it was like to be treated like a child.

Henry and Veronica took a long walk around the camp. Sabrina feared they would bicker again, but when they returned, they were hand in hand. They looked the way Sabrina always remembered them—happily in love.

By evening, everyone ran out of ways to keep themselves busy, and they were dying for news from the army. The family sat together in the mess tent, quietly picking through beef stew and corn bread, when Red Riding Hood and Mr. Canis entered. It was clear the little girl had been crying—perhaps it was due to another startling memory.

"I remembered the Master's face," she said.

"You did?!" Sabrina cried, hopefully.

Mr. Canis shook his head. "Not entirely."

"I remember that the face was unusual. It changed a lot. Sometimes it was scary, and sometimes it was kind."

"Like he has two heads?" Sabrina asked, her curiosity piqued.

"That's all she's remembered so far," Mr. Canis said. "We're going to stop for the evening. The toll on the child is too much."

Granny took Red into her arms. "You are very brave, *liebling*."

"I'm trying." Red sighed.

Sabrina, however, was irritated. Didn't Red understand how important it was to uncover the identity of the Master? Why was it so hard to remember his face?

A frantic guard rushed into the tent. "The soldiers! They're back!"

Everyone rushed into the courtyard just as the massive fort gates swung open. Sabrina was expecting another defeated crowd, but instead, a triumphant fleet of soldiers marched into the camp, cheering, singing, and carrying Prince Charming on their shoulders.

"We destroyed the marina!" Snow White announced to the Grimms. "We took them completely by surprise." She, too, was suddenly lifted onto a troll's shoulders and paraded through the camp.

"The marina?" Henry exclaimed. "I thought the plan called for an attack on the sheriff's office."

"That's what we all thought, but once we marched out of camp this morning, Charming changed his mind," Rip Van Winkle reported. "The man is a genius."

"William, we're confused," Granny Relda called to the prince.

"Well, Relda, we have good news and bad news," he replied, jumping down from his perch. "The good news is, we just cut off a very important supply line for the Master. The bad news is that we have a traitor within our ranks. Someone in this camp fed our battle plans directly to the Scarlet Hand. I suspected it all along, and it proved true today."

"I was at Nottingham's office," Goldilocks chimed in. "The entire Scarlet Hand army was there waiting for us. If we had gone there, we probably wouldn't have come back."

"So, you went to the marina to finish the original plan!" Daphne cried. "Gravy!"

"Exactly. The Hand never saw us coming," Charming said, puffing out his chest proudly. "I suspect our saboteur and our spy are the same person. We now urgently need to find out who that person is, before they can do any more damage."

"Worry about it tomorrow!" Snow crowed. "These people need to celebrate. We showed the Master, didn't we?"

The crowd roared.

"Have a little fun. You deserve it!" she cried.

Tables were conjured, candles were lit, and wine flowed freely. There was dancing and singing, and soldiers shared battle stories that grew more exaggerated with each telling. Sabrina spotted Morgan le Fay and Mr. Seven dancing beside the supply tent. He was standing on a chair so the two could be cheek to cheek.

Snow was right, everyone needed a little celebration, but Sabrina couldn't help worrying about the spy. There were hundreds of Everafters in the camp, many of whom she didn't know at all. Any one of them could be working against the army.

"I wonder what the spy has planned for us tonight," she grumbled to her family.

Granny shook her head. "It's a terrible shame that someone would turn on their own people."

"It could be anyone," Daphne said. "Did anyone find any clues?"

Uncle Jake shook his head. "I searched the garden more thoroughly this morning. There was nothing there."

"The chicken coop was a total bust," Daphne said.

"I've been so worried about the refugees that I forgot to go back to the armory," Sabrina admitted.

"I searched it myself," Henry said. "There were no clues, but I suspect whoever broke all those arrows came in through the window. They must have been little."

Suddenly, Sabrina remembered the little wooden object that had caused her to fall in the armory. She dug it out of her pocket and showed it to the group.

"I found this thing," she said.

Everyone grew quiet. Sabrina herself was so surprised, she could barely speak.

"It's a little leg," Granny said.

"A little wooden leg," Veronica said, picking it up and examining it.

"It looks like one of Pinocchio's marionette legs," Daphne added.

"How did it end up in the armory?" Sabrina asked, but the looks on her family members' faces told her the answer.

"It can't be him," Granny said.

"It can totally be him," Uncle Jake said.

"What other explanation would there be?" Mr. Canis said. "He showed up out of nowhere. We don't know where he's been, who he's been talking to, or why he came back."

"Wait! You really think Pinocchio is the spy?" Sabrina asked.

Granny's face fell. "Poor Geppetto. He'll be heartbroken."

"What do we do?" Veronica asked. "Should we confront him?"

Mr. Canis stood without a word and hobbled toward Pinocchio's tent. Everyone followed. He used his cane to lift the tent's flap. Inside were a hundred finished marionettes, along with several thick blocks of wood and a carving knife. On one wall of the tent shone a bloodred handprint.

The old man searched through the marionettes until he found one with a missing leg. The one Sabrina had found in the armory fit perfectly. He tossed both pieces angrily to the ground.

"Anybody have any doubts now?" Henry asked.

"It appears the party is over," a voice called. Pinocchio stood in the doorway.

Sabrina spun on him. "Explain yourself!" she growled.

"The Master came to me with an offer I couldn't refuse. He's going to help me correct the Blue Fairy's mistake. Soon, I will abandon this childish form and finally be a man."

"And it doesn't matter to you that you're putting the rest of us in grave danger?" she asked. "Your father is here. What if he gets killed because of the things you are doing?"

"My father is safe! The Master has made that promise to me. Oh, don't look at me with such shock. Do you have any idea what it's like to be seen and spoken to as a child every day?"

"Uh, yeah?" Daphne snapped.

"Try it for hundreds of years! Never allowed to grow up because

I am trapped in this little boy's body. The Blue Fairy thought she was giving me a gift, but look how she has cursed me. The Master will correct this injustice."

"And if people die in the process?" Uncle Jake cried. He snatched the boy by the collar and pushed him against the wall of the tent.

"That's entirely up to you, Jacob. You don't have to be his enemy," Pinocchio said. "The Master can be your friend. He can give you anything you want. You could wish your princess back to life, and he would make it happen. All you have to do is give up your fight."

"You're disgusting. Your friend killed the woman I love!"

Granny stepped forward and tried to calm her son, but Jake refused to back down.

"He's just a boy," she said.

"No, Mom, he's not! You heard him. He's a monster!" Jake shouted.

"Where do we put him so he can't cause any more trouble?" Henry asked.

Before anyone could answer, a horrible roar filled the air and shook the walls of the tent. Sabrina recognized the sound.

"Dragon!" she cried.

Panic rose up throughout the camp. Through the doorway, Sabrina saw people running around frantically, screaming and crying. Everafters were trampling one another in the melee. Knights sprinted through the courtyard with swords drawn. In the madness, Pinocchio pulled free from Jake. He darted out into the crowds, disappearing from sight.

Puck was eager to chase after Pinocchio, but Granny stopped him. "We'll catch him later. Right now, we have to help everyone to safety."

The family raced out from the tent. Charming was outside, climbing atop a table with his sword in hand. "Get to your posts. Remember your training. We can fight this thing!"

A violet-colored dragon with the face of a cat appeared on the horizon. It circled the camp like a vulture preparing to feast.

"Three just swooped over the fort," Robin Hood shouted, pointing north. "But I think there are at least ten in total. One blasted the west wall. I sent guards to put out the fire, but the water tower valve is broken. There's no way to get any water to the hoses or the cannons."

Granny Relda took a deep, steadying breath. "Veronica, I seem to remember you were pretty good with mechanical gizmos."

"I've fixed a few leaky sinks in my day," Veronica said.

"You're the best we've got. Get over to the water tower and see if you can't get those valves working."

Veronica raced off to do what she could.

"Henry, get up to the east tower and switch that water cannon on," Granny Relda said. "As soon as Veronica has the water working, try to knock those dragons out of the air."

"But the girls—"

"Henry, they'll be fine," she reassured him. "Besides, I've got a job for them that will keep them safe. Trust me."

Henry still looked worried, but he nodded. The conversation he'd had with Sabrina seemed to make a difference. It was clear that trusting his daughters didn't come naturally to him, especially when there was danger, but somehow he forced himself to let go. He raced off to do as he was told.

Puck took his sword from his belt. "All right, well, I guess I have to go up there and kill some flying iguanas," he said with a grin.

"Actually, I need you to help the girls, and it's a job only a mischievous juvenile delinquent like yourself can do. How do you feel about throwing some rocks?" the old woman asked.

Puck grimaced. "I hardly think a few rocks will take down a dragon."

Granny pointed behind her at one of Boarman and Swineheart's catapults. A giant boulder was already loaded into its arm. Several more sat nearby.

Puck rubbed his hands together eagerly. "I'm in."

Canis stepped forward. "Relda, perhaps it's time to bring the Wolf back to the fight. I believe I now have the ability to control him, and I have the jar in my—"

"Absolutely not, old friend," she scolded. "We can manage without that monster. Besides, I'm going to need you and Red to get me through this camp once it's safe."

Everyone raced to do their jobs. Sabrina studied the catapult closely. Despite its crude appearance, it was incredibly complex. It had dozens of knobs and buttons as well as an intricate series of weights and counterweights. Puck aimed it while Sabrina and Daphne pushed buttons and pulled ropes. When a black dragon with white tusks buzzed past the fortress, Sabrina shouted for Puck to fire, but he refused.

"We have to wait until it's lined up perfectly," he said. "Don't worry. We'll get another chance."

"I don't want another chance. Just shoot the thing down," Sabrina said. "It's coming right at us!"

The dragon made a beeline for the catapult. Once it was close enough, it reared back and prepared to blast them with its fiery breath. Puck gave the order, and Daphne slammed her hand down on a red button. The giant spring inside the machine screeched, and, with incredible force, the arm of the catapult whipped upward. The boulder rocketed into the sky.

"Eat that, ugly!" Puck cried as the boulder slammed into the dragon's face. The beast bellowed in agony, and magma poured from the wound. The creature fell out of the sky and slammed into the courtyard. Its eyes closed, and its heaving chest grew still.

"That's one!" Puck crowed, celebrating with a ridiculous victory dance.

"Nine to go!" Sabrina said as she pulled the levers to lower the catapult's arm. "We need to reload. You think you can pull that off?"

Puck spun on his heels and transformed into an enormous elephant. He lumbered over to the nearest boulder and pushed against it with his head. The huge stone rolled slowly forward. It was clearly an effort for Puck, even in this state, but he pushed onward until the rock sat firmly in the catapult's arm.

The girls fiddled away at the knobs and weights once more. While they worked, Sabrina watched her father in the east tower. The cannon he maneuvered was fed by the water tower, but with the valve busted it was useless. As a brown dragon flew by, it blasted the exterior wall of the camp. Helpless, Henry could not put out the flames. When the dragon doubled back and buzzed past the top of the watchtower, Henry was forced to duck low to avoid its black talons.

"How's it going, Mom?" Sabrina shouted, panicking.

Veronica stood atop a ladder near the tower and was trying to pull something out of the gears. "Pinocchio shoved something in here. If I could only get it out, the water will come . . ."

"Could you hurry?" Henry shouted from across the camp.

"Keep your pants on, Hank!" she cried.

The brown dragon pivoted in the sky and flew like an arrow at Henry's watchtower. He was a sitting duck.

"Puck, we have to get the brown one now!" Sabrina screamed.

Puck transformed back to his regular state and then turned the catapult in the proper direction. He looked through a scope to line up his shot.

"Puck, don't miss," Sabrina said fiercely.

"I won't miss," Puck snapped back. "Fire!"

Daphne slammed the red button, and another rock flew into the sky. It rocketed past the monster and flew into the forest.

"Oops," Puck said.

Sabrina looked up and saw the dragon preparing his blast. Her father stood, cornered, on the tower. There was nothing she could do.

"I got it!" Veronica cried, and, suddenly, water was blasting out of the cannon directly into the mouth of the dragon. It gurgled and gasped as it fell to the ground, dead.

"That was the coolest thing I've ever seen!" Puck cried as he ran for the other watchtower. "You guys handle the rock thrower. I'm going to have fun with the big squirt gun!"

"Hey! How are we supposed to load this thing?" Sabrina cried after him, but the fairy boy was already gone.

Daphne looked over at the next boulder. "There's no way we can lift that thing. Even together."

"You help Dad. I'll go get Puck," Sabrina said, and the girls raced off in opposite directions. Soon, Sabrina reached the platform where Puck was busy spraying water all over the forest, ignoring the circling monsters.

"You really have an attention problem," Sabrina said, pointing to a jade-colored dragon looming toward them. She wrenched the cannon from Puck and turned it toward the monster. She pushed the firing button lightly, just to see how much water would come out, and was surprised to see a flood blast from the nozzle. As the dragon got closer, she braced herself and fired. The water shot out of the cannon and hit the dragon right in the jaw. It was a lucky but effective shot, and the creature reared back in panic.

"Hey! I saw the squirt gun first! Go kill dragons with something else," Puck shouted as he shoved Sabrina out of the way. A white dragon appeared on his left and barreled down on the fort, shooting a blast of flame that left a scorched trail across the courtyard and ignited the far wall.

"You're not supposed to let them burn the place to the ground!" Sabrina shrieked. "If you can't do this, step aside."

Puck growled. "Leave me alone. I know what I'm doing."

He fired the cannon but didn't aim very well. The white dragon was unfazed and continued circling the fort.

"Give me the cannon, Puck," Sabrina said, pushing the boy out of the way. Once she was in control, she searched the skies for the flying menace. She soon spotted the same white dragon approaching fast. She trained the weapon on the beast and waited patiently. She needed to let it get closer in order to blast it with enough force to kill it. In fact, to get the best shot, she needed it to be nearly on top of her. Though her brain was telling her to run, she grasped the handle of the cannon tightly and forced herself to stay put. *Closer. Closer.* She could feel the heat of the creature approaching. Her ears were full of its roars and beating wings. *Let it get closer. Any second!* When she couldn't wait another second, she fired right into the dragon's open jaws. It fell out of the sky, crashing inside the camp and leveling the mess tent. It skidded across the yard, slamming into another dead dragon.

"Lucky shot!" Puck complained as he snatched the cannon away again. He spun it toward another approaching monster and fired, missing the mark completely. He tried again and again but failed every time.

"What's the matter, booger brain? Do you need a bigger target?" Sabrina mocked, pulling the cannon away from him.

He yanked it back. "I probably can't hit anything because you've infected me with your puberty virus."

"Puck, puberty isn't a virus. You go through it when you grow up."

"Well, I'm an Everafter. I don't grow up!" he shouted. "I'm perfectly happy to stay this age forever, but you came along, and now all of a sudden I'm getting taller and my voice is changing. It's all your fault!"

"Don't look at me. I didn't ask you to grow up," Sabrina said, scanning the sky for more dragons.

Just then, three arrows thudded into the side of the platform. Sabrina ducked and scanned the forest for their source. She nearly fell over in shock when she spotted the massive army approaching. There must have been two thousand Everafters marching in their direction. Sheriff Nottingham and the Queen of Hearts led the throng.

"The Scarlet Hand is here!" Sabrina shouted down to the soldiers inside the camp. The news caused the panic to escalate, and many fled into cabins and tents, choosing to hide rather than fight. She snatched the cannon back from Puck and turned it on the approaching forces. It unleashed a typhoon of water, knocking nearly a hundred goblin soldiers flat. She didn't let up, showering the villains mercilessly and leveling another five hundred before the water unexpectedly turned into a trickle.

She turned to the water tower where her mother was peering into a glass window on its side.

"It's run dry!" she shouted. "We're out of water."

"That can't be right! You must be doing it wrong," Puck said. He pushed the FIRE button over and over with no results. "You broke it!"

He swung the cannon around in anger, and the nozzle hit Sabrina in the chest, knocking her off the platform. How ironic, she thought, as she fell to her certain death, that at that moment she would have given anything to be a giant goose again.

9

AIR RUSHED PAST SABRINA'S BODY AS SHE plummeted to the ground, but, suddenly, she felt a tingling on her back, and she was no longer falling. Instead, she was hanging upside down, inches from the ground. A long, furry tail stuck out of the back of her pants. It was wrapped around one of the tower's beams and kept her dangling like a yo-yo.

Puck flew down to her.

"Look what you did to me with your stupid pranks. I have a tail!" she raged.

She expected him to cackle with glee, but Puck's face was trembling. "I'm sorry."

"What?" Sabrina said blankly. She wasn't sure she'd heard him correctly.

"I almost killed you," he said, rubbing his teary eyes on his

filthy hoodie. He was deeply troubled. He gently freed her and placed her safely on the ground.

"Since when do you care?" Sabrina asked.

Prince Charming and Snow White rushed to their side. "We . . . we have to retreat. Get your family and go."

"Retreat? To where?" Sabrina asked.

"There are too many dragons, and their army is too big," Charming said. "Sabrina, I think we should herd everyone into the Hall of Wonders."

Mr. Canis, Red Riding Hood, and Daphne appeared with Elvis, Granny Relda, Henry, and Veronica.

"Agreed," Granny said,

"But what about . . . ?" Daphne trailed off anxiously, pointing to the dragon still fighting Arthur's knights in the center of the camp. It was blocking the entrance to Charming's cabin.

Puck's wings unfurled. "I'll handle it," he said.

"I thought you weren't the hero type," Sabrina challenged.

"I'm not, but you make it impossible to stay a villain," Puck said, then turned to Granny Relda. "Old lady, if I die, I'd like you to do one small thing for me. I want you to build a one-hundred-acre museum dedicated to my memory. Have at least three hundred marble statues erected of me in my most dashing poses. One of these statues should stand one hundred feet tall and greet ships as they float down the Hudson River. One of the wings of the museum should house an amusement park with the world's fastest roller coaster. None of the rides should be equipped with safety devices. You can rent some of the space to fast-food restaurants and ice-cream parlors, but nothing should be healthy or nutritious. The gift shop can sell Puck dolls packed with broken glass and asbestos. There's a more detailed list in my room."

He flapped his wings and rose into the air.

"Puck, I absolutely forbid this!" Granny cried.

"You're going to get yourself killed," Sabrina said.

"I have this covered, Grimm. I'll be fine," he said, waving his wooden sword in the air.

"That's a toy!" she shouted.

"Don't disrespect the sword!" he cried, and then he shot toward the dragon. He jabbed it in the ear, and the monster roared. It turned its massive body toward Puck and exhaled. A ball of fire as big as a car rocketed toward him. He dodged it, but only narrowly.

"Missed me, ugly?" Puck taunted, soaring up higher into the sky. The angry dragon growled and followed.

With the path clear, the Grimms hurried into Charming's cabin. Once inside, they found the magic mirrors leaning against the wall. Harry and Reggie were waiting in the reflections, looking alarmed.

"What is all that racket?" Harry asked.

"Sounds like war has broken out," Reggie said.

"Yes, it has. Harry, we're coming through. Tell Mirror he's going to get some visitors," Henry explained.

"Oh, dear. Hurry, folks, you'll be safe inside," Harry promised.

Henry and the family helped the elderly Everafters through the reflection first and then the very young and the smaller animals. One by one, the frightened refugees stepped through, but more continued to arrive when they heard Snow's call for retreat. Geppetto was one of them, racing into the cabin in a panic.

"Have you seen my boy?" he begged.

Granny bit her lip. "He's already in the mirror," she lied.

Geppetto thanked her and raced through the reflection.

Granny sighed. "I just couldn't tell him the truth."

Prince Charming rushed into the cabin, dragging Snow with him.

"Ms. White! I won't hear another word of this. Get through the portal, now!"

Snow stomped her foot. "Mr. Charming, as you may know, I am not seven years old. I can take care of myself."

"Fine, you want to be difficult?" Charming threw up his hands in frustration. "This is a direct order from your commanding officer. Sergeant White, you are to get into the Hall of Wonders at once."

Snow looked up at him as if she were seeing him for the first time. Her anger melted away, and she did as he asked.

"If you don't come through in five minutes, I'm coming back for you," she promised.

"Boss, why aren't you housing the refugees in the hotel? We have plenty of rooms available," Harry asked.

"My hotel?!" Charming growled. "These mongrels would destroy the place. The sheets are five hundred thread count."

Reggie looked nervous. "I suppose the Island of Wonders is out of the question, too, then? All well and good, but Beauty lent me to you with the belief that you would keep me safe. I'm fragile, you know."

"Yeah, boss. You can't just leave us here," Harry said. "Wait, do I hear dragons?"

"Can I take a magic mirror into a magic mirror?" the prince asked.

Reggie shrugged.

Harry scratched his head. "There's nothing in my instruction book about it, I'm afraid."

"Has it ever been tried before?" Charming asked impatiently.

"No, sir," Harry said.

"But listen, man, you're messin' wit' serious mojo here," Reggie cried. "You don't want to play around wit' t'ings you don't understand."

Charming took Reggie off the wall and pushed his mirror into Henry's hands. "Hank, take this with you."

"Oh, I get to mess with the serious mojo?" Henry asked, looking skeptical, but Charming had already bolted out of the cabin and back into the fray before he could argue.

"What about me?" Harry cried.

Sabrina heard the popping and snapping of burning timber. Smoke drifted into the cabin and irritated her nose and eyes. The camp was burning.

"We need to get everyone into the hall now," Veronica cried. She did her best to hurry the steady stream of refugees through Harry's reflection, but a bottleneck of panicked Everafters clogged the portals and slowed everything down. Still, Veronica got them through, sometimes shoving roughly to get them moving. One after another, they disappeared through the reflection until the only people left were King Arthur's knights, a few brave princes, and most of the Merry Men.

"Where's Jacob?" Granny Relda cried.

"He's at Briar's grave," King Arthur reported. "He refuses to leave."

Henry gave Reggie to Arthur, and, before anyone could stop him, he darted out of the cabin after his brother. Sabrina raced after him. They zigzagged across the courtyard as bombs exploded left and right. One eruption was so close that it knocked Sabrina off her feet and rattled her brain. Her father helped her to her feet, and they kept running until they found Jake standing over Briar's grave.

"You have to come, Jake," Henry said.

"I won't leave her," Uncle Jake said.

"You have to. Do you want to join her?"

"Maybe I do, Hank."

Sabrina gasped. "That isn't what Briar would want," she said.

"What would you know about what she would want?" Jake snapped. "You didn't love her, Sabrina. You don't know anything about her."

"I knew her!" Sabrina shouted over the noise. "She wouldn't want you to stay here and die. She was a fighter. She would want you to fight, too."

Tears escaped her uncle's eyes.

"You're not alone, Jake," Henry said. "I'm here. Mom's here. The girls are here. We're going to help you get through this, but right now we have to go!"

Uncle Jake leaned down and picked a rosebud from the magical bush and put it into one of his many pockets, right over his heart.

"OK," he said, sounding defeated. He turned, and together the three Grimms raced back to Charming's cabin. They arrived just in time to see Mr. Canis and Red Riding Hood stepping into the mirror. Arthur handed Reggie back to Henry, who followed Veronica through the reflection.

As if on cue, Charming returned.

"What are you waiting for? Get into the hall, now!" Charming shouted. "The Hand has broken through the gate. They're swarming the camp."

Everyone tumbled into Harry's reflection and raced through the portal. Mirror was waiting for them in the Room of Reflections.

"I've got to go back for Harry," Mirror said. He was leaping into action, when there was a massive crash. Sabrina turned back to the portal to the Hotel of Wonders and saw Sheriff Nottingham on the other side. He was holding a heavy sledgehammer high above his head. He swung it down as hard as he could, slamming it into Harry's reflection.

Harry appeared, looking terrified.

"He's trying to break me," Harry said.

"Uh-oh!" Daphne said.

"Didn't you say that when a mirror is broken, everything inside it is cut to ribbons?" Sabrina asked Mirror.

"Boss, what can I do?" Harry called to Charming, desperately.

"Harry, there's a box in room nineteen. It's in the bureau and very important. Can you fetch it for me?"

"Of course, sir. In a jiffy," Harry said, then vanished.

"Let's go out there and help him," Arthur said, but as if on cue, a mob of goblins and trolls stormed into the cabin. They were wielding horrible weapons and eager for a fight.

"They'll kill us," Henry said.

"We have to do something," Sabrina shouted as Nottingham pounded on the reflection again.

"Billy?" Snow said. "What should we do?"

Charming said nothing. He stared into the reflection, watching the sheriff do his ugly work.

"We can't just stand here," Daphne cried.

Another blow hit the mirror, and a tiny crack appeared in the reflection.

"Harry!" Charming muttered as he wrung his hands. "C'mon, Harry!"

Several long seconds passed; then Harry reappeared. Charming slipped his hand through the mirror and took the small black box. It was tiny, barely large enough to hold a ring.

"Here you go, boss. Did I do OK, boss?"

"You did very well, Harry," Charming said.

"Harry, can you step through into our mirror?" Daphne asked.

Harry flashed a melancholy smile. "I'm sorry, little one. But I'm afraid that *is* in the instruction book. I can't leave my mirror."

A ripple of cracks rolled across the glass, distorting Harry's face.

"It was fun, boss," Harry said to the prince.

Charming nodded. "Indeed it was."

"Aloha, my friends," Harry said, just as Nottingham's sledgehammer smacked the reflection one final time. A fiery-red handprint appeared at the center of the glass, identical to the one Sabrina saw appear when the Wicked Queen had threatened to "fix" Mirror not long ago. It burned bright and hot, and then the reflection shattered. A million pieces spilled out of the frame and onto the floor. Harry and his Hotel of Wonders were gone.

Charming stared at the broken shards for a moment as he stuffed the black box into his suit jacket. His jaw was clenched, hard and tight.

"I'm sorry," Sabrina said to him. "I know Harry was a friend."

Charming shook his head. "Harry was not real. I can't mourn him."

"But—"

"What about Puck?" Sabrina asked, suddenly remembering he was still out in the camp fighting the dragon.

Granny looked worried. "I'm sure he'll be all right, Sabrina."

Sabrina wasn't sure she believed her.

Meanwhile, the crowd was on the verge of panic. Many were injured. Nurse Sprat was busy dressing their wounds, but there were too many for her to handle. Even with Granny, Veronica, and Goldilocks's combined help, people continued to suffer. Worse still, it was clear their numbers had dwindled. More than half the camp did not make it into the hall.

Charming raised his hand for attention, and the crowd turned to him.

"Battles are won. Battles are lost. But for the sake of those who fell, we fight on. I know that as you look around, a feeling of discouragement wells up in your throats. But you need to spit that feeling out on the floor. Stomp on it. Smash it into dust. It has no place here. We will fight again, and we will show the Master and his Hand how discouragement feels."

"We've had enough of your pep talks, Charming," Mr. Boarman cried. "People died today, and a lot of pretty words aren't going to make us feel better about it."

Little Bo Peep stepped forward. "We cannot beat the Scarlet Hand."

Charming tried to speak again, but he was booed into silence.

Then, Mr. Seven stepped forward. "We are already beating them!" the little man shouted over the crowd. Everyone turned to find Mr. Seven standing with Morgan La Fay. His face was determined and strong. "You want to know why those dragons were sent after us? Because we're a threat! The Master is furious that we took the marina. He's enraged because we cut off his supply line. And we did it all while a spy told him our every move."

"A spy!" Rapunzel cried.

"Yes, we are all under surveillance by a member of the Scarlet Hand, and we still managed to beat them. Even though we're outnumbered, we scared the Master so badly, he sent his most vicious weapons to wipe us out. And they couldn't get the job done. He took some of our friends, but we took out four dragons. Plus, I'm told Sabrina Grimm wiped out hundreds of his soldiers all by herself. That is astounding, people. We're doing what the Hand thought was impossible. We're surviving! Do you hear me? We're surviving! And the next time we see his ugly army, we're going to beat them again!"

The crowd roared. Many danced and sang; others hugged and kissed one another. Seven was so caught up in the celebration, he kissed Morgan on the mouth. The woman looked surprised but happy.

Sabrina was stunned as she watched the refugees.

"Perhaps Mr. Seven is the charming one," Granny Relda said.

The crowd shouted and shook swords, wands, and fists in the air. They lifted Seven off the ground and marched him around on their shoulders.

As the Grimms watched the celebration, Charming approached them. "I'm told Geppetto's boy was responsible for the sabotage."

"Unfortunately, yes," Granny replied. "He escaped when we confronted him. I fear he may have been killed by the dragons."

Charming looked around at the impromptu celebration. "Or he's hiding in this crowd. We'll catch him eventually."

Henry stepped forward. "You've got a bigger problem than that, Prince. Bringing the troops inside the Hall of Wonders might have saved their lives, but I'm afraid we're all stuck in here. There's an army blocking both exits."

"We're not trapped at all, Henry," the prince replied. "We're going to march right out the front door."

Henry shook his head in disbelief.

Nurse Sprat appeared. "Excuse me, I don't mean to interrupt, but I was hoping I could borrow Veronica and the girls."

"Of course," Veronica said, and then turned to Henry. "We'll be right back. Will you save me a dance?"

Henry kissed her. "I'll save them all for you."

Veronica, Sabrina, and Daphne followed the nurse through the crowd. Once they were safely out of earshot, Sprat turned to the group and took Veronica's hands in her own. Her expression was serious and troubled. "I have some bad news—"

"It's the baby," Veronica interrupted. Her hand glided across her belly.

"You are not pregnant," Nurse Sprat confirmed, "anymore."

A tear rolled down Veronica's cheek, and she looked to Sabrina and then Daphne. "I'm sorry, girls."

The girls hugged her tightly, as if they could fight back the sadness.

"Oh, now, wait! Veronica, you didn't lose the baby," the nurse said. "This is so confusing. I don't even understand it, really. That's why I brought in some help."

Morgan le Fay approached. "Sorry I'm late. I got a little side-tracked."

Nurse Sprat nodded. "Did you bring your magic?"

"I never leave home without it," the witch said, waving her hands in the air. A blue mist materialized and swirled around Veronica.

"Nurse Sprat, what is this all about?" Veronica asked, startled.

"Just a moment," the nurse replied. She watched the vapor as it changed colors from blue to red. Then, it vanished.

"Just as you suspected, Nurse," Morgan le Fay said. "Something magical happened to Veronica."

"Can someone please tell us what's going on?" Sabrina snapped.

"Veronica, it's just a theory, but—"

"Just tell me," Veronica begged.

"You were pregnant. Even though you were asleep at the time, the baby grew at a normal pace. It was healthy, and you took it to term."

"I'm not sure what you're telling me," Veronica said.

"I found something unusual in your blood sample, a peculiar compound I have never seen before," the nurse said. "But it was clearly magical."

"That's where I came in. Nurse Sprat let me take a look, and it's definitely Donnoga Root," Morgan said. "It was used back in the old country by women who were expecting difficult births—you know, human-giant infants, frog-princess hybrids, things of that nature. Beauty and the Beast used it, as did Ms. Muffet and the Spider. It makes would-be-impossible births possible."

"And this Nooganar Root was in my blood?" Veronica asked.

"Donnoga Root," Nurse Sprat said. "We found traces in the sample. Someone used it on you."

Daphne stepped forward. "But, my mom wasn't having an impossible birth. She was having a normal baby."

"A normal baby," Sprat explained, "but not a normal birth. Your mother was asleep and under a magical spell. She wouldn't have been able to give birth if she was entirely unconscious, so the herb helped with the birth. Whoever did this—"

"They took my baby!" Veronica cried. Her voice shook with panic.

Sabrina wanted to tell her mother that was crazy, but she knew better. She remembered the crib in Red Riding Hood's room at the mental hospital. She heard a child crying in the halls. The little lunatic called him her baby brother. Then, there was the Wizard of Oz, who said her parents were giving birth to a new future. There were hints and clues all around them, all along, and she'd never understood them. But why? What did the Master need with her baby brother, and where was he now? There was only one person who could tell her.

"Where's Red Riding Hood?" Sabrina snapped.

"With Mr. Canis, I think," Daphne said. "Why?"

Sabrina ran back to the crowd. "Let me by!" she shouted as she pushed through their celebration. "I need to get past!"

She soon spotted Mr. Canis and Red Riding Hood. The little girl wore a smile on her face and was enjoying the festivities. Sabrina ran to her and snatched her by the cloak.

"Where is the baby?" she demanded.

"What baby?" Red asked, feebly.

"Don't play dumb with me. I know you have him," Sabrina said. She had never been so angry and so afraid in her whole life.

"I don't know what you're talking about," Red shouted.

"Sabrina, leave her alone," Mr. Canis demanded, but she ignored him.

"Think, Red. You took the baby, and he's somewhere in that stupid head of yours," Sabrina said. "You better remember, or I will shake the truth out of you."

Red pulled away. "I'm trying!"

"Sabrina, that's enough," Canis shouted, again.

Sabrina reeled on him. "You make her remember! She and the Master stole my baby brother. She knows where he is."

Veronica and Daphne raced to join them.

"Sabrina, stop this," Veronica said.

"She knows where he is, Mom," Sabrina repeated. "She took him!"

"I'm sorry. I'm so sorry. I wasn't myself," Red said through streaming tears. She cowered, as if worried Sabrina might hit her.

"So, you remember it now?" Sabrina snapped.

There was a moment of clarity in Red's eyes, as if something were rising out of the muck of her memories to the surface.

"There was a crib . . . in a room with holes in the walls," Red said. "Little holes that let him see us, little holes that let him see what I was doing. The baby is there, now. He keeps it close as he watches us all."

"Who is *he*? Who is the Master?"

Red Riding Hood looked into Sabrina's eyes. Sabrina could see the little girl's struggle. Red knew this was important, but she could not get at it. It was locked down too deep.

Veronica took Sabrina and Daphne into her arms. They held each other and cried. There was nothing else to do.

10

EVERYONE TOOK THE TROLLEY BACK TO THE house, ready to storm the Hand, only to find that the mob was gone. All that remained were hundreds of broken spears and arrows and one abandoned cannon. The house had not been harmed, though the front yard was a disaster.

"The Master must have sent everyone to attack the camp," Snow said.

"He threw everything he had at us," Morgan le Fay added.

This automatic victory was good news for the refugees, raising their spirits even more than Mr. Seven's heroic speech. Charming had promoted him to general, and the little man marched the soldiers through the Grimms' house and out the front door. The family watched strangers and friends file past, wishing them well.

"Where are you headed?" Sabrina asked Buzzflower.

"Well, we've been told the plan is to take Town Hall, but I'm not sure that's where we're actually headed," Buzzflower said. "This fight has been full of surprises."

"Sergeant White says all we need to know is how to fight, not where it's going to happen," Mallobarb added.

Uncle Jake joined them. "May I march with you, ladies?"

"You can't go, Jacob. It's too dangerous," Granny cried.

"We'll look after him," Mallobarb said. "He's family now."

Uncle Jake walked ahead, leaving his real family behind.

"We might never see him again," Veronica said, fighting back tears.

"We'll see him again," Daphne said. "He's Uncle Jake. He's gravy."

Goldilocks and the three bears were the next to file out the door.

"Goldie, are you sure you have to go?" Granny asked. "There's plenty of room here, and the fighting is only going to get worse."

Goldilocks shook her head. "I've been avoiding my responsibilities for too long, Relda."

Veronica stepped forward. "Goldie, if you're doing this to avoid me . . . you can't risk life and limb because you think it will be uncomfortable here. It won't be—you are more than welcome to stay."

"You're amazing, Veronica. I'm not sure you meant what you just said, but you said it nonetheless. I doubt I would have done the same," Goldie replied. She stole a look at Henry and shrugged. "Take care of this one, Henry. She's a keeper."

Soon, all the soldiers were gone and the family was alone. They stood in the front yard watching the last of the army disappear down the road and silently thanking their good luck. Somehow, they had survived an army of bloodthirsty villains, complete with a fleet of fire-breathing dragons.

They were enjoying the well-earned peace and quiet when, suddenly, something massive fell out of the sky and landed in the front yard. The impact was so powerful that everyone lost their footing and fell to the ground. When Sabrina scrambled back to her feet, she saw a white dragon lying dead in the front yard. Puck floated down from the sky and landed on its belly. He waved his wooden sword at her.

"Don't disrespect the sword, Grimm," Puck said with a smirk.

The first order of business was getting the water and electricity working. Puck reattached the severed electrical lines to the pole, and for the rest of the day his hair stood on end. Veronica worked her own brand of magic on the water pipes. Everyone else opened windows and took out rotting garbage that had been sitting in the hot house for five days.

There wasn't much still edible in the refrigerator, but Granny made a feast consisting of what appeared to be fried oysters in peanut butter and jelly sauce. Sabrina could barely handle the smell.

"I ate her cooking for eighteen years," Henry whispered. "You get used to it."

"Oh, yeah, when?"

"I think it happened when I was seventeen," he admitted.

The entire table burst into laughter. Granny Relda was offended at first, but she soon joined in and eventually laughed the hardest of all.

The rest of meal, they all told jokes and stories. For what seemed like the first time since they woke up, Sabrina's parents weren't fighting. Sabrina looked around the table at her family: Mom, Dad, Granny Relda, Daphne, Puck, Mr. Canis, and Red Riding Hood. She realized this was what she had been hoping for all along. If only the whole family was there—namely, Uncle Jake and her baby brother. Where was the baby? Was he safe? She looked over to her mother and from her worried expression could see she was wondering the same thing. Somehow, they had to find him.

"So, Henry," Puck said as he kicked off his shoes and propped his smelly feet up on the kitchen table. "I was wondering what you can tell me about puberty."

Sabrina wanted to crawl under the table and die.

Sabrina was getting ready for bed when Daphne came into the room carrying her pillow.

"Are you back?" Sabrina asked, hopefully.

"Not by choice," the little girl grumbled. "Granny kicked me out of her room. She says I snore. That's the pot calling the kettle black!"

"I missed you," Sabrina admitted.

"I know. Think about that feeling the next time you want to lie to me," her sister said as she opened the desk drawer. From it, she removed a hairbrush and then crawled up behind Sabrina and began brushing her hair.

"You know, I'm very proud to be your sister," Sabrina said.

"Gravy."

Sabrina smiled. "Gravy."

"But if we're going to be sisters again, there has to be a new rule. No more talk about going back to Manhattan. Our baby brother is here somewhere, and we have to find him. All of our friends are in danger, including Uncle Jake. We can't leave."

"I know," Sabrina said.

"No grumbling about it, either," the little girl added.

"No promises."

"Hey, where are those marionettes?" Daphne asked, glancing at the dresser. "Didn't you say Dad brought them in here?"

"He threw them out," Sabrina said. "I saw him toss them into the trash bin in the kitchen. After what Pinocchio did, I don't think Dad wanted them around."

"Good," Daphne said. "They were creepy anyway."

"Super creepy. Puppets give me the willies," Sabrina said. She crawled under the covers, and Daphne did the same. She felt the little girl's hand slide into her own. It felt good to have her sister back. Soon, both girls were asleep.

Sometime during the night, Sabrina woke up. The clock on the nightstand read 3:00 A.M. She padded to the bathroom for a drink of water. When she turned to go back to her room, something was blocking her path. One of Pinocchio's marionettes was sitting in the middle of the hallway. She nearly screamed but then guessed it was another of Puck's pranks. He would definitely dig through the trash to have some fun at her expense.

"That's hilarious, Puck," she said. "I thought our war was over."

She scooped the marionette off the floor and stuffed it into the bathroom trash can. Then, she went back to bed.

She wasn't under the covers longer than ten minutes when she heard someone shuffling across her bedroom floor. She sat up and flipped on the light. There, on her dressing room table, was the marionette.

"Aargh!" she cried, which woke Daphne.

"What's going on?" Daphne grumbled.

"Puck's being a jerk," she said. "C'mon."

Sabrina snatched up the puppet, and the two sisters pounded on Puck's door until he answered. He was wearing a pair of footie pajamas decorated with happy cowboys. He was half-asleep and annoyed. "Whatever you're selling, I'm not interested."

"What's the big idea?" Daphne said.

"I don't know what you're talking about," Puck said.

Sabrina shook the marionette at Puck. "You keep trying to spook me with this!"

"You've got the wrong prankster. Boys don't play with dolls."

"Don't you sleep with a stuffed unicorn?" Daphne said.

Puck stuck his tongue out and slammed the door in their faces.

"Stop goofing off, freak boy," Sabrina shouted.

Puck's bedroom door opened again. "It wasn't me. You can send your apology in writing." He slammed the door in their faces again.

Sabrina tossed the puppet into the hall trash, and together she and Daphne headed back to their room. They complained about having to live with the king of stupid pranks for a while before drifting off to sleep.

Once again, it didn't last. Sabrina woke to find Daphne's hand clamped over her mouth. Daphne was pointing at the dresser on the other side of the room.

Sabrina peered into the dark and nearly screamed. The marionette was back, along with all the others Pinocchio had made, but they weren't sitting on the dressing table. They were walking around the room under their own power. They opened the dresser drawers and rooted through the girls' still-packed suitcases. One searched the closet, while others scurried around under their bed.

"Did you know they could do that?" Daphne mouthed the words.

Sabrina shook her head.

"What are they looking for?"

Sabrina shrugged. She turned back and saw her own mario-nette rummaging through the desk.

"I found them," it squeaked, holding up Sabrina's enormous set of keys. The weight of the keys made the creature stumble onto the floor, but it quickly righted itself.

"Let's go. The boss is waiting," the Granny Relda marionette commanded, and all the others followed her out into the hallway.

"What are they doing?" Daphne whispered.

"We're going to find out," Sabrina said, pulling her sister out of bed. Together, they crept into the hallway just in time to watch the marionettes unlock Mirror's room.

Just then, Henry and Veronica joined them.

"Did you see them, too?" Veronica asked.

"You mean the walking, talking marionettes?" Sabrina asked. "Yeah, we saw them. They stole my Hall of Wonders keys."

"We'll get Mr. Canis and your grandmother," Henry said. "You wake up Puck."

The girls pounded on Puck's door for what seemed like forever. When he finally opened up, his stuffed unicorn was tucked under his arm. "You two are really pushing your luck," Puck said. "What is so important?"

"The creepy puppets are alive," Sabrina said.

"OK, that counts," he said, tossing his unicorn aside and pushing past them. He hurried into Mirror's room with the girls on his heels.

"Let's go get them," Puck said.

"We should wait for the others," Daphne said.

"For a bunch of puppets?" Puck scoffed. "We can take care of this. C'mon!"

Sabrina agreed and led the others through the reflection. On the other side, they found the Grimm marionettes, as well as a hundred more, passing out Sabrina's keys to one another.

"If we're quiet, we can sneak up on them," Puck whispered. But his voice still echoed off the walls and bounced around like a basketball. In unison, all of the marionettes turned their heads toward them. They sprang into action, racing down the hallway and unlocking doors as they went.

"What is this all about?" Daphne asked her sister.

Sabrina didn't have a clue, but she was starting to panic. Most of the doors hid rooms filled with useful weapons and gizmos the family used frequently, but, farther down, in the direction the marionettes were heading, there were terrible things—things that should not be let loose.

"We have to stop this," Sabrina cried, but it was too late. Just as she said the words, a door opened, and out stomped a huge blue ox. It was as big as a Winnebago and had enormous horns on either side of its head. It stomped a front leg angrily and lowered its head toward the girls.

"That's Paul Bunyan's ox, Babe," Sabrina said.

"That's the coolest thing I've ever seen," Puck said.

"How cool is it going to be when it stomps us to death?" Sabrina said.

"Considerably less cool," Puck replied. "Run!"

The three children turned to flee and heard the beast bellow as it started after them. The trio leaped through the portal, but that didn't stop the ox. The creature crashed into the real world as the mirror increased in size to accommodate its massive body. Unfortunately, Granny's house didn't have the same magical ability, and the animal caused an incredible amount of damage. It knocked through the wall that faced the lawn and tore through the roof with one of its huge horns. The confined space seemed to make it panic, and it whipped its head around, wreaking even more destruction. When it stomped its feet, the floor collapsed. The ox fell into the living room below. The children stood on a thin ledge of what was once the bedroom floor, looking down at the chaos below. Sabrina saw her family standing downstairs, looking up at them.

"It appears we have a problem, Relda," Mr. Canis said.

"Open the front door," Granny said, and the old man did as he was told. Like the mirror, the front door morphed to allow the ox out, and it stomped onto the front lawn. But that was not the end of the chaos. A giant three-headed dog tumbled out of the mirror next, and it immediately fell through the hole in the floor.

"There's something you don't see every day," Puck said.

The dog was followed by a wave of bizarre beasties and monsters. Snakes with heads on both ends of their bodies slithered out. People who looked like zombies, vampires, and werewolves from horror movies did the same. There was a seven-foot albino man with stringy muscles and pink eyes. There were pirates, wizards, witches, and unearthly creatures that looked like they were from other planets. They came through the portal, wave after wave after wave, as if being pushed forward by an even bigger crowd behind them. Creatures made from ice and fire, a man surrounded by his own tornado, and a headless rider sitting atop a black horse. All the family could do was watch the macabre parade as it went by. Each creature fell into the pit then stumbled outside to freedom.

When the last of the creatures came through and a few peaceful seconds had passed, Sabrina, Daphne, and Puck carefully edged toward the magic mirror.

"Kids, just stay where you are," Henry called. "I'll get a ladder and help you down."

"We have to check on Mirror," Daphne said.

"It's not safe," Veronica said.

"He's part of our family, Mom," Sabrina said. "We'll be careful."

The children headed into the reflection. Inside the Hall of Wonders, Sabrina saw that every door was flung open wide. The marionettes were nowhere to be seen, and neither was Mirror.

"Mirror!" Sabrina shouted, but the little man did not respond.

"We can't go from room to room looking for him. It would take forever," Daphne said.

"The trolley isn't here. If he's alive, he's probably at the other end of the hall," Sabrina said.

Puck's wings expanded. He hoisted the girls into the air. He flew them down the hallway so fast that the open doors along the way slammed shut. In no time at all, he came to rest outside the closed door to the Room of Reflections.

Sabrina pushed the heavy door open and looked inside, but Mirror wasn't there. The room was empty except for the magic mirrors hanging on the wall.

"Maybe one of the monsters ate him," Daphne whimpered.

"That would be awesome," Puck said.

Sabrina flashed him an angry look.

"Awesome in a terrible, heartbreakingly tragic kind of way," Puck continued.

In a panic, Sabrina spun back around, determined to search every room until they found their friend. As she dashed out of the Room of Reflections, she heard someone talking.

"Do you hear that?" she asked the others.

Both Puck and Daphne nodded.

She turned back toward the Room of Reflections, trying to follow the sound. It was clearly coming from inside the room, which was empty except for the mirrors.

Daphne walked around the perimeter of the room, listening closely at each of the unbroken mirrors. "It's not coming from these."

Sabrina agreed. "It seems to be coming from the door." She pushed it shut, closing them inside the room. That's when she spotted the passageway the open door had hidden all along.

"What's this?" Daphne asked.

Sabrina shrugged and stepped through the arch. There, she saw Pinocchio, surrounded by his evil marionettes, standing in front of a wall with thousands of pieces of broken mirrors glued to it. None of them reflected anything; rather, they acted like windows into places all over town and beyond. A quick glance showed her Nottingham's office, Mayor Heart's study, Jack the Giant Killer's empty apartment, even the Wizard of Oz's workroom at Macy's in Manhattan. Mayor Heart was staring through one, as were the Frog Prince and many other members of the Scarlet Hand.

"Have the doors been opened in the Grimm home, Master?" Mayor Heart said from one of the shards.

"You're the Master?!" Daphne shouted in disbelief at Pinocchio.

Pinocchio turned just as Daphne kicked him in the shin. The little boy howled and fell over. His marionettes leaped to his defense, jumping on Daphne's back and punching her. It took all of Sabrina and Puck's effort to free her from the tiny villains.

"Do you know the nightmare you have inflicted on my family? You're a horrible, evil worm," Sabrina shouted at the boy.

"I'm not the Master!" Pinocchio groaned as he held his wounded leg.

"Then what's with the evil lair?" Puck said.

"It's not his. It's mine," a familiar voice said behind them. "I am the Master."

Sabrina spun around. Mirror was standing in the shadows, holding a little boy in his arms. A horrible mixture of terror, betrayal, shock, and disgust filled Sabrina's head and heart. One moment she wanted to run—to put as much distance between herself and Mirror as possible. The next, she wanted to snatch him by the collar and shake him in fury until he explained himself.

"No. That can't be," Daphne whispered.

"You? You're the Master? You're the leader of the Scarlet Hand?" Sabrina said.

Mirror nodded his head slightly. "Yes."

"But you—" Daphne said, trembling.

"But I was your friend? Is that what you were going to say?"

"Yes! I trusted you. We all trusted you!" Sabrina cried.

"Then I'm afraid you've made a terrible mistake," Mirror said.

Enraged, Sabrina ran at Mirror, but a bolt of lightning stopped her in her tracks. She knew the kind of magic Mirror controlled, but never had it been directed at her.

"I don't want to hurt you, Sabrina," he said.

Sabrina studied the boy in Mirror's arms. He was small, maybe a year and a half old. His curly red hair was the same shade as her grandmother's locks. He had Sabrina's father's face and her mother's beautiful eyes. "That's my brother. You took him," Sabrina spat.

Mirror nodded. "I can explain it all, Sabrina, but right now I have a wish to fulfill. Are you ready, Pinocchio?"

"I am," the boy said, bowing respectfully.

"Very good," Mirror said, then turned to the girls. "I'll be needing your help."

"Help doing what?" Daphne asked.

"Follow me," he said. He led them back into the hall until they reached an oak door. Sabrina recognized it immediately. The door had two round stones set in its front, each with a sunken relief of a handprint—no keyhole and no plaque. "I need you to unlock this."

Sabrina scanned it again. She still couldn't find a keyhole.

"That's not possible," Sabrina said. "There's no keyhole, and, besides, I don't have a key."

"Child, you and your sister *are* the keys," Mirror said.

"I think Charming is right about you," Daphne said. "You're defective."

Mirror huffed impatiently.

"This room has a special lock—one that can only be opened by a Grimm," Mirror explained as he set the baby in Pinocchio's arms. "I hoped Junior could do it for me, but it seems I need two members of your family."

"Whatever is in there is staying in there," Sabrina said. "We won't open it."

Mirror roughly snatched the girls and forced their hands onto the handprints. A warm, pleasant sensation came over Sabrina, like stepping out of a snowstorm into a toasty room. A chime rang in her ears, and the stone sank into the door. It triggered an orchestra of moving parts—internal locks and tumblers, a burst of steam that hissed from the cracks around the door, and, finally, a heavy *clunk!*

The door swung open. Mirror smiled wide and barged into the room, pulling Sabrina behind him. Most of the other rooms in the Hall of Wonders were overflowing with magical items or wild, fantastical creatures. This room, however, was completely empty except for an old, leather-bound book resting on a thin wooden stand.

Mirror caressed the book's cover lovingly. "After eons of wishing and praying, you are finally mine."

"Well, I guess we can relax. All Mr. Baldy wanted was a book," Puck said. "I gotta tell you, Mirror, this is the most boring evil plan in the history of evil plans."

"This isn't just any old book. This is the Book of Everafter."

"Sorry. I haven't read it. I'm waiting for the movie," Puck said.

Mirror scowled. "It's the only one of its kind—a collection of stories about Everafters. Every fairy tale, folk story, and tall tale ever told is in these pages."

"But it's more than that, isn't it?" Sabrina said. Even across the room, she could feel the tickle of magic coming from the book.

"It's a second chance at a happy ending, Sabrina," Mirror said. He then turned to Pinocchio. He took the baby boy from him and gestured to the book. "You did well, boy, and I promised you a reward."

"What do I need to do?" Pinocchio asked.

"Your story is in this book. Find it and change it to whatever you please. When you return to us, the changes will become reality. Your story will be rewritten, and so will you."

"Wait! You're saying he can go into his story and rewrite it? To change his own history?" Sabrina said. "That's impossible."

Mirror shook his head in disappointment. "Sabrina, with everything you've seen in this town, I would think you would know better by now. Nothing is impossible in Ferryport Landing."

Pinocchio rubbed his hands together eagerly. "Let's get started. What do I do?"

"I'm told it's as simple as flipping it open," Mirror said, handing the boy the huge book.

Pinocchio didn't hesitate. He snatched the book away and opened it. A bright light shone from the pages as they rapidly flipped back and forth.

"I will never be able to find my story if it doesn't slow down," Pinocchio whined.

"You have to find your story, Pinocchio. It won't put you there automatically, but there are doors that lead you from fable to fable," Mirror shouted over the wind.

Pinocchio looked uncertain. He slipped his hand into the whirling pages, and—in a flash—he was gone. His marionettes chased after him, diving into the pages as if they were going for a swim.

"And now it's my turn to change my story," Mirror said, shifting the baby in his arms.

"Not a chance," Puck said, and then he stepped between Mirror and the book. Mirror fired an electrical blast from his fingertips, and it hit the ground at Puck's feet, knocking him aside.

"Don't take the baby, Mirror. He's got nothing to do with this," Sabrina begged.

"Oh, he's got everything to do with this."

"You're a traitor!" Sabrina yelled.

Mirror frowned. He looked genuinely hurt. "I'm not expecting you to understand, but try to imagine what my life has been like—trapped in this hall for eternity, bought and sold to the highest bidder like property, serving the whims of others."

"We treated you well!" Sabrina shouted. "You were our friend."

"No amount of kindness is a substitute for freedom. I'm going into the Book of Everafter, and I'm coming out a free man."

"You can't go in there," Sabrina said. "You can't leave the Hall of Wonders."

"I'm not leaving the Hall of Wonders," Mirror said with a sly grin. "The book will be here the whole time."

"But you'll still be stuck in Ferryport Landing," Daphne argued.

Mirror looked down at the child.

"Not if I'm in a human body," he said. He placed his hands into the whipping pages, and he and the baby vanished.

"He's lost his mind," Puck said, finally climbing to his feet.

"No he hasn't," Sabrina said, fiercely. "He knows exactly what he's doing. It was his plan all along. He kidnapped our parents the moment he learned Mom was pregnant. Then, he took the baby and kept it safe until he could get us to open this room. Now he's going to go into the book to change his story—I think so that his mind is in control of our baby brother."

"But how?" Daphne cried.

"I don't know, but we have to stop him," Sabrina said.

"We're not going in there," Puck said, eyeing the power still blasting out of the book.

"Yeah, this is one of those times we should definitely wait for an adult's help," Daphne said.

"Everyone is at the other end of the hall without the trolley. It will take hours to get them and get back," Sabrina argued. "Mirror could already be in his story, making the changes. He could be stealing the baby's body as we speak. We have to do this ourselves."

Daphne reached out and took Sabrina's hand, and then she took Puck's. He scowled but held on anyway.

"Every time I try to get out of the hero business, you pull me back in!"

The trio stepped toward the book.

"Any idea which story we'll land in first?" Daphne asked.

Sabrina shook her head. "Just pray it's not something insane. Some of these fairy tales are totally nuts."

Sabrina put her hand on one of the book's pages. There was an odd sensation, like being flushed down a toilet, and then everything went black.

When the lights came on, Sabrina looked down and then around. She was lying on the dirt floor of a wooden farmhouse. Her sister was safe and sound on a bed, wearing a yellow dress. Puck was nowhere to be found.

"Where's Puck?"

"Maybe he didn't make it." Daphne shrugged. "What story is this?"

Sabrina went to the door and opened it a crack. In the yard was a sea of little people. Right outside the door was a road made entirely of yellow bricks. She groaned.

"Not here," she grumbled.

"Let me see," Daphne said, and she pushed past her sister.

Their presence sent a cheer through the crowd, and the Munchkins rushed forward and lifted them both onto their tiny shoulders.

"You killed the Wicked Witch of the East," one of the Munchkins cried. "You saved us all."

Sabrina turned and saw a pair of legs jutting out from beneath the tiny farmhouse. They were wearing a pair of shiny silver shoes with a ruby-red tint to them.

"Daphne, I don't think we're in Ferryport Landing anymore."

ENJOY THIS
SNEAK PEEK FROM

8

THE SISTERS GRIMM

~ THE INSIDE STORY ~

1

I DON'T THINK WE'RE IN FERRYPORT LANDING ANY-more," Sabrina said to her sister, Daphne.

The sisters Grimm were trapped inside a shabby farmhouse, and they were completely surrounded.

"They're singing for us," Daphne said, looking outside.

"Get away from the window," Sabrina scolded.

Like their surroundings, Daphne had changed. Gone were her overalls and sneakers. Instead, she wore a yellow dress. She smiled brightly, her eyes filled with curiosity as she peered outside. There, the girls found hundreds of little faces staring back at them.

"We're in Oz, aren't we?" Daphne exclaimed.

Sabrina studied the road leading away from the house. It was paved with yellow bricks.

"This is so awesome!" Daphne squealed.

"No, Daphne, it's not awesome. Everyone from Oz is crazy!"

"They're just unusual. I can't believe it! I didn't believe Mirror at first, but look! We're inside a real-live fairy tale!"

At the mention of Mirror, a wave of sadness swept over Sabrina. Her throat tightened, and she fought back tears. She felt betrayed, heartbroken, and confused. She never wanted to hear his name again.

"I wonder when Dorothy will show up," Daphne mused.

"Try to focus," Sabrina insisted. "We jumped into this book to save our baby brother. We don't have time to waste with some idiot from Kansas. We need to come up with a plan."

There was a knock at the door.

"Maybe we should start with opening the door?" Daphne suggested.

Sabrina sat down on one of the creaky beds. "They can wait. I . . . I really don't know what to do."

"I'm sorry," Daphne said, "but did the great Sabrina Grimm just say she didn't have a plan?"

Sabrina knew her sister was teasing, but she couldn't crack a smile. She was completely at a loss for ideas.

"Well, we can't just sit here all day. Maybe the Munchkins have seen Mirror and our brother. They could point us in the right direction," Daphne said as she opened the door.

Three men and a little old lady were waiting for them. They smiled brightly. "Welcome—" the woman started, but Sabrina jumped up and slammed the door in her face.

"We can't just barrel into this without thinking," she snapped. "It could be dangerous. If the Book of Everafter really does have every fairy tale ever told, then it's filled with some really nasty monsters and murderers."

"So we'll kick butt and take names like we always do," the little girl said matter-of-factly before opening the door again. The old lady and her friends were waiting, looking confused.

"Welcome—" the woman started hopefully, only to have Sabrina slam the door in her face again.

"This isn't the real world, Daphne. This book has its own rules. Like that dress you're wearing—you didn't have that on when we jumped into these pages. Where did it come from?"

Daphne looked down at the yellow dress. "Why did it change my clothes and leave you alone?"

Sabrina was still wearing her jeans and sweater. "It's weird."

"Well, big sister, Granny Relda says the only way to solve a mystery is to jump right in." She reached for the door again.

Sabrina groaned. "Fine! But stay close. And just so you know, I have no problem serving up a plate of knuckle sandwiches to these weirdoes!"

"Be nice," Daphne insisted, opening the door once more.

"Welcome!" the old lady said quickly, bracing herself for the door.

"Hi!" Daphne said.

The crowd of Munchkins in the square gaped in wonder and let out a collective "Oooohhhhhhhh!"

The woman bowed deeply. "You are welcome, most noble Sorceress, to the land of the Munchkins. We are so grateful to you for—"

"No problem," Sabrina interrupted, rolling her eyes at Daphne. "So, we're looking for a man traveling with a little boy. Has anyone seen them?"

The Munchkins seemed startled by her response.

"You are welcome, most noble Sorceress, to the land of the Munchkins. We are so grateful to you for having killed the Wicked Witch of the East and for setting our people free from bondage," the old woman recited again.

"I told you, they're nuts!" Sabrina growled.

"Wait a minute! We killed who?" Daphne shouted. She pushed through the crowd, grabbing Sabrina's hand and dragging her along. The duo found a pair of feet wearing silver shoes sticking out from under the farmhouse.

"Oh no!" Sabrina cried.

"Someone call nine-one-one!" Daphne shouted. She knelt next to the feet. "Lady? Are you OK? I'm sorry we dropped a house on you."

One of the tiny men stepped forward. "Child, that's not the line. Are you attempting to alter the story?"

Sabrina and Daphne shared a confused glance. "Huh?"

The woman leaned in close and whispered, "That's not what you are supposed to say. You have to ask me if I'm a Munchkin."

Sabrina scowled and clenched her fists. "Can we save the stupid games for later? There's a woman trapped under this house, and—"

"Wait!" Daphne interrupted. "Are you telling us we have to say the lines from the story? Why?"

One of the men stepped forward and whispered, "If you don't, you'll attract the Editor."

"And the Editor is bad?" Daphne whispered back.

The man nodded. "Very bad."

"OK, we'll try. Are you a Munchkin?" Daphne asked.

The woman sighed with great relief. "No, but I am their friend. When they saw the Wicked Witch of the East was dead, the Munchkins sent a swift messenger to me, and I came at once. I am the Witch of the North."

"Wrong! Glinda is the Witch of the North," Sabrina sneered.

Daphne shook her head. "That's in the movie. Glinda's the Witch of the South. Haven't you read the book?"

"I only skimmed it," Sabrina admitted.

Another of the little men chimed in quietly. "No, you're supposed to say, 'Oh, gracious! Are you a real witch?'"

Sabrina stamped her foot and fumed. "Just let me punch *one* of them," she begged her sister. "It will be a lesson for the others."

"Silence your animal, Dorothy!" another Munchkin snapped at Daphne. "She's going to get us all into trouble."

"Did you just call me an animal?" Sabrina growled.

"Dorothy?" Daphne said. "You think I'm Dorothy?"

The Munchkin nodded. "You were assigned the role when you entered the tale, and you must play along. Or, there will be grave consequences for us all!"

Daphne beamed. "I'm Dorothy! That explains the dress."

"Dorothy's dress is blue," Sabrina argued.

"Nope, that's the movie," Daphne said.

"Whatever. If you're Dorothy, then who did the book turn me into?" Sabrina asked, looking down at herself for some clue.

Daphne snickered and pointed to Sabrina's neck. "You're not going to like the answer."

Sabrina found she was wearing a small leather collar with a silver tag. The name TOTO was engraved in the metal. She threw it to the ground in anger. "Of course! I have to be the dog!"

Daphne laughed so hard, she snorted.

"Keep laughing," Sabrina fumed. "Just don't be surprised if I bite you."

ABOUT THE AUTHOR

Michael Buckley is the *New York Times* bestselling author of the Sisters Grimm and NERDS series, *Kel Gilligan's Daredevil Stunt Show*, and the Undertow Trilogy. He has also written and developed television shows for many networks. Michael lives in Brooklyn, New York, with his wife, Alison; their son, Finn; and their dog, Friday.